REVEALED

Jeni Burns

Revealed

Twisted Fate Novella #3

Copyright © 2015

Jeni Burns

c/o Media Jam, LLC

15105-D John J. Delaney Drive; #317

Charlotte, NC 28277

Cover Design By: Valentine Pinova

Print ISBNs
ISBN: 1-942964-08-0
ISBN-13: 978-1-942964-08-7

Acknowledgements:

With every book I think there are even more people than the last to thank. I tend to get dreadfully long-winded, so I'll try to keep it short and sweet this time around.

Thanks to my family who loves me even when I forget to move the clean laundry from the washer to the dryer and still insist that I'm the best mom and wife they've ever had. I try to not think about the fact that I'm their only mom and wife.

A shout-out to the fantastic folks at Rush Espresso in Ballantyne for putting up with my decaf coffee and poached eggs habit.

On that same coffee-related note, a huge shout-out to the amazing Sophia Henry who meets me for coffee and makes my back cover blurbs sound good without having to read the story. Oh, and for understanding that writing with you makes me a stronger writer. You inspire me. I'm so proud of you and all you've accomplished.

To Reagan Phillips for pushing me to be better every day than I was the one before. Your texts, emails, and dinners out keep me working. I'm so lucky to have you and I can't wait to read your next book.

To Denise Leton, who lets me plot all my killings over cheese fries with bacon on her lunch hour and then insists on reading all my awful drafts because she's the best critique partner on the planet. Oh, and for sending me the best and most appreciated texts on the planet to fuel my muse's creativity.

To N.R. Ratcliffe for indulging my antics both on the page and off. I love having you as my partner in crime.

To Adrienne Trent and the fantastic group of writers at Carolina Romance Writers (CRW). They inspire me to work smarter, not harder and be the best writer I can be today. Then they make me try harder tomorrow.

A huge thank you to Lara Stokes, Jamie Pejo, and Lauriel Faltin, beta readers extraordinaire. I work to surprise you with each novella. A special added thank you to Lauriel Faltin for naming this book. Trust me, what I was thinking of was horrible. She's the reason the title is good.

Thank you to Valentine Pinova for the cover art.

A huge thank you to everyone who helped edit including, Jan Carol, Help Me Edit Editing Services, and Joshua Strecker. Without these amazingly talented professionals, I'd still be rocking in a corner wondering where the commas go.

And last, but surely not least, thank you to all my friends and family who have stood behind me and cheered me along this journey. To Taz Shahpurwala who will meet me for a beer even if we live over 500 miles apart to listen to me worry about the next book and Dee Lorenzo for calling daily to ask me when the next book will be ready because she's tired of waiting. You ladies drive me. A special thank you to George Lauer for letting me call you with story ideas, male dialogue, and frustrated tears and then giving me a much needed virtual hug and sending me back to work. I'd be lost without your friendship.

With all my thanks,
~ j

To Lara Stokes.

For loving my characters as much as I do.

Or, maybe even more.

Jeni Burns

ONE

"HAVE YOU READ today's missed connections?" Callie Dewsberry asked in way of greeting when her oldest and dearest friend trudged through the door of The Daily Dews, her family's occult bookstore slash coffee shop.

"You know I didn't. I never do. And yet, you still ask," retorted Daphne as she pulled out the seat opposite her.

"You really should read it. I'm almost positive this post is about you." Callie slid the paper across the table and nearly knocked over her steaming cup of heaven.

"Before I read that," Daphne said and motioned to the paper, "I need some of that." She pointed at the cup.

"Here, take mine. I'll make another." Being an only child had always made her wonder how she'd manage sharing her life with someone some day, but then she looked at Daphne and realized that with a friend like her, she would be A-okay.

She watched her friend take a tentative sip of the coffee and moan with orgasmic bliss. It never ceased to surprise her just how the dark liquid could make someone so happy.

"Is this the new blend?"

"You know it is. The beans are chocolate infused and aged in an oak container." Pride crept into her voice. There were only two things she was passionate about in life. One was coffee and the other was singing. In fact, if she had her way, she'd drop everything and run off to New York City to audition her way into a Broadway show. But then she'd be leaving her grandparents in the lurch.

The Daily Dews had been in the family as long as recorded town history. It hadn't always been an occult bookstore, but the witchy rumors that went along with the business gave her a sense of pride. There was something interesting about being tied to one of the many paranormal musings around town, and at least gave her a point of excitement since she wasn't working her way toward fame and fortune on Broadway.

"Okay, so which one of these screams my name to you?"

"Oh, yeah. This one." Callie ran her finger down the newsprint until the word "beguiling" caught her eye. "This is the one." She tapped the ad twice for emphasis.

Daphne scanned the ad then gave her a puzzled look. "Okay, so I'll bite. What made you think this was about me?"

"'Beguiling brunette in the hardware store looking at drywall Spackle,'" Callie read aloud. "Who else can that be? I mean how many brunettes spend their time in hardware stores looking at drywall supplies?" Callie paused for a beat before continuing. "Only you. That's who." She leveled a pointed look at her friend and waited for the argument she knew would follow. It always did.

"If this ad is meant for a man, then the number goes *way* up," Daphne argued.

"Pish posh. You and I both know that you're beguiling — and any man in his right mind would want to chat you up."

"Okay, so if that's the case, then why didn't he just say something?"

"Because you're also intimidating as hell, Daph." Callie rolled her eyes and got up to get herself a fresh cup of coffee. "Want another?" she offered as the fresh scent wafted through the air.

"Of course," Daphne replied, slurping down the rest of her cup. "And since when am I intimidating?"

A snort escaped before Callie could rein it in. "Daphne Barren. Are you seriously asking me when you got the rep for being intimidating?" She laughed aloud. "You've been intimidating poor boys since you joined the public world."

A dubious look graced her friend's hauntingly beautiful face. "Don't you remember that poor boy who stuttered his whole freshman year in high school until he got the nerve to ask you out for the Spring Fling?"

"Stewart?"

"That's his name." In her excitement, hot liquid splashed over the top of the cups she was carrying and scalded her skin. "He was never the same again after you turned him down." She set the cups down and wiped her hands on her jeans.

"Ugh. In my defense, he barely came up to my shoulders, Cal. Remember? It was because of him I decided to make a minimum height requirement." Daphne arched an eyebrow and waved her hands over her curvy figure. "Six-two and taller to ride this ride, remember?"

3

Callie tucked her legs under her butt, settling into the chair. "Oh, I remember all right. Pretty sure Stewart does too. Poor guy never spoke again after all," she waved her hands at Daphne's chest, "*that*."

"Fair enough. But why would some guy think some strange girl would even answer one of these ads? I mean, is he so desperate that he needs to take out an ad to get a date? And if so, what does it say for the woman who actually answers him?"

Callie ducked her head and blew on her hot coffee so her long-time friend wouldn't see the redness that crept up her face. If Daphne flat out asked her, she wouldn't lie to her, but the embarrassment of what she'd done might just kill her.

"So, back to drywall, are you still free this afternoon?" Daphne folded the paper over and moved it aside.

"Yeah, Grams is gonna come in for a bit so I can leave early." The hot coffee washed away her shame. If only her friend knew that the man who had written the ad would be waiting here tomorrow morning to meet his missed connection. At the time, writing him back had seemed reasonable. Oh well, like so many of Daphne's rejects, Callie would let this one down easy.

"Dax'll be there." Daphne gave her best contrite look.

"Daph, you know I have no interest in seeing your brother."

"But Nic'll be there too. Does that make it better?"

"No. Nic stopped talking to me when Dax and I started dating again. And now that we've broken up, I'm sure it'll be all sorts of fun being in the same room with both of them." She shook her head.

4

Hanging drywall was going to suck enough, but hanging drywall between two of the most handsome men she knew was just plain torture. Dax, Nic, and Daphne were triplets, and they all shared stunning good looks. Triple sets of piercing blue eyes, dark hair, and chiseled cheekbones with skin that glowed crystalline. Of the three, Daphne was the most striking, but Dax's bad boy, sleep-tussled looks, and inked arms sent her heart racing. And then there was Nic. Quiet and shy, with eyes that could see into her soul if she dared meet his gaze for more than a moment. Warmth spread through her veins and pooled low in her belly. She shook the thoughts away. Daphne was waving her hands with the excitement of a recaptured thought.

"You know, I was down at the hall of records yesterday and found all sorts of old articles about the house. Did you know that back in the early 1800's there was a scandal there with the owner?"

Callie did her best to look interested in her friend's musings, but the old Victorian didn't register in her brain as anything more than a money pit, no matter how much Daphne dreamed of a B&B.

"Ever since I started sleeping there, weird things have been happening."

And Callie was back, full attention on each careful word Daphne spoke. "You didn't tell me that. What's happened?"

"One night I swear something was messing with my sheets."

"How so?" Nerve endings sprang to life at the base of her skull. It wasn't often she got to explore the fun side of owning the only occult resource in all of northern New Jersey.

"Well, I woke up around two in the morning and I swear to you, someone was sliding the covers off me from the bottom of the bed."

"Are you sure you didn't kick the covers off and they were just falling?" Ever since an encounter with a mystical being years ago, Daphne was always looking around corners for something out of the normal; something shy of earthly.

"I'm sure. And then this morning, when I got out of the shower, there were streaks in the mirror. You know, like when someone writes something in the steam?" An expectant look settled in her sapphire eyes.

"Well, how about I come over and do a sage cleanse while the boys work on the drywall?" Callie offered. It would do wonders for a house as old as Daph's new place and she could dodge Dax and Nic. Two birds, one stone.

"I still need you to help me hang drywall," Daphne whined. "You *all* promised you'd help do my room, remember? I wanted my suite to be our project. As a family. The contractors are done with the rest of the place, which means we need to finish my suite so I can get the occupant permit in time for the soft opening."

"Hey, I remember telling you that I'd paint. I don't know the first thing about hanging drywall." Callie tapped her index finger on the table for emphasis. "I'm more of the tear-shit-down, not put-stuff-up type of gal."

"Oh, come on. The contractor showed me how to do it. It's not that hard," Daphne insisted.

"That's what she said."

Daphne swatted Callie's arm as their laughter echoed through the empty store.

"You're ridiculous." Daphne shook her head as the laughter died off. "It's not *difficult*. Besides, I'm not sure I can manage my brothers alone."

"Okay. I'll be there with sage and if I can dispel your haunt before they finish the damn walls, I'll try not to break anything."

"That's all I'm asking."

Smug wasn't a good color on her friend, but it fit her perfectly. Now if Callie could just come up with enough excuses to keep her away from the guys, all would be fine.

TWO

DRAMMELECH WAITED IMPATIENTLY in the woods. One would think that something of his origins wouldn't need to spend his time waiting around for a human, but here he was, and the damn human was late. Again.

Heavy boots crunched through the underbrush behind him signaling the arrival of the one man that might be convinced to join him in his quest for greatness.

"Thirteen." The voice was lower than it had been almost thirteen years ago, now that puberty had left a lasting impression on the full-grown man before him.

"Might as well call me Elech. Your father does now." He waved a dismissive hand and continued. "You conjured?" Annoyance coated his every word.

"I'm here to propose a deal," the young man simply stated as he tucked a helmet under his arm. "But this time, you won't mess with my family."

He was a cheeky bastard. A mere human thinking he had the power to call forth a devil and make demands. Ha.

"Do you forget who you address? I've walked this plane for almost three hundred years. I'm certain good ol' Donovan will tell you that making a deal with me will cost you exactly what I think is appropriate and nothing more or less." He cracked his knuckles and gave his best impersonation of a smile. "Your family is my family, boy. Don't let the stories your father spews complicate things." Drammelech leaned against a nearby tree and felt it tremble under his weight. Even the foliage knew to fear him.

"My father screwed everything up. He promised you my sister and gave you my mother. His soul will one day be yours. How much worse could it get?"

"Oh, my dear boy." His chuckle roared into full-fledged laughter. "You have so much to learn." His patience waned with every passing moment. "Tell me why I'm here."

"I want my mother back." The whine that accompanied the request only illustrated the ignorance of the man.

"I cannot return something that was freely given to me."

"But she didn't know you'd take it while she was still alive." The man shuffled his feet, kicking up dirt and debris.

Elech could see the boy still deep inside the man before him in his movements. It was true he was a grown man, but when it came to his mother, the man was still a lost little boy, and that worked in Elech's favor when it came to getting what he needed.

"True, but would that have really changed her offer?"

"Of course it would've." The man stopped fidgeting and stared. "My mother would never have given up her life for what my father did if she knew it meant she would be taken from us that night."

"Maybe. Maybe not." Drammelech stroked his chin and contemplated Hope's son. "I have an idea. There's a pendant that will allow you to talk to her. Then you can ask her yourself what her choice would've been."

Drammelech watched confusion take root in the man's face. "Your sister wears one." He arched a brow as recognition dawned on the man's face. "And I'm sure there are others that match it." A slight nod from the man was the only confirmation that Drammelech needed.

"So, that's all I have to do? No signing over my soul? No promising my firstborn?"

"A pendant is all I need. If you desire more, then we can discuss the value of your soul." He waved a finger in the man's direction. "Although in it's present condition it isn't worth as much as you might think." He shook his head and tapped the dual tips of his tongue on his teeth.

This was going to be a hell of a lot easier than he thought. Drammelech turned his back on the man and disappeared into the woods, dreaming of all he would accomplish with one little piece of witchy jewelry.

★★★★★

Dax Barren watched the retreating figure of his family's nemesis. Did people really have such things? Probably only those who made a deal with a damn devil. He shook his head and considered his options. Thirteen knowing about Daphne's pendant was an interesting turn of events.

That necklace was the last thing their mother had given her before he'd taken her soul right out of her body and left her an empty shell of a human. A shell that rotted away hooked up to machines. If he knew his sister, it would take an act of God to get her to remove the pendant from her body. Dax couldn't remember a time since that horrible night that Daphne had gone without the gift hung around her neck.

A chime sounded in his jeans pocket. He withdrew the sleek cell and silenced the digital reminder before hiking back to the road where his Streetfighter waited. The motorcycle glistened in the sun, but for the first time since buying it, riding held little appeal. Maybe it was because he realized he didn't need something that would get him someplace fast, but a place to actually go. Someplace with a warm embrace waiting just for him.

His cell vibrated and sang as soon as he had his helmet in place. A quick look at the screen told him all he needed to know: he was late and Daphne was impatient. Rather than risk being any later, he pocketed the cell and revved the bike's engine.

Light traffic on the back roads that led from Harmony to Belvidere made it possible to pull into Daph's driveway less than ten minutes after her call. It wasn't until he rounded the house and jumped over the front porch railing that he noticed the white pickup parked at the curb. His heart flip-flopped and his feet stopped mid stride.

"Where the heck were you? I told you to be here at four." His sister's whine could peel paint off the walls when she really tried — and this was one of those times. She stood in the threshold of the front door of her soon-to-be bed and breakfast.

"I told you I'd be here and here I am." He took one last glance at the truck and wondered how he'd missed it on his way in. Shit, this was going to be harder than hefting sheets of drywall for the next few hours.

"Yeah, but you're late and Nic is starting without you. You know it'll be crooked if someone doesn't help him."

"Can't Callie help him?" He shot his sister a pointed look and she had the good grace to feign a sheepish grimace in response. "Why didn't you tell me she was gonna be here?"

"Get over it, Dax. That was so last year." Daphne padded out onto the porch in her bare feet and looped her arm through his. "I'm sure she doesn't even remember why you two stopped talking, so why keep avoiding her?"

"You know damn well she remembers. And so do I."

She lowered her voice as they neared the front door of the house. "Look, I know you both said some stupid stuff, and then you did that thing that we won't discuss with that woman that will remain nameless for the rest of today. Mmm-kay?"

"Sure. Let's just get this done and over with," he grumbled as she pulled him over the threshold.

The old Victorian had been a pit the first time he'd seen it months ago, but like everything his sister touched, it had evolved into something magical. The floors shined like new and every wall boasted a fresh coat of paint. The most impressive piece was the restored picture window. It had been the selling point for his sister. After she had seen it, his sister couldn't be talked out of putting all her hard earned cash into this place.

"Isn't it beautiful? The artisan that restored it did a fabulous job."

"It's…" He grappled for a word to fit the scene captured in the colored glass pane. A forlorn lover pining after a woman that should be a pane over, but was eerily absent. "Something. That's for sure."

"Dax!" She swatted his arm. A crash from somewhere above them sent her running up the stairs. "Nic, I told you to wait for me," she yelled.

His sister was pretty damn bossy for being the youngest. He turned back to the window and gave a small salute to the man forever entrapped in the glass.

"He looks so sad."

The musical voice of Calliope Dewsberry made him jump and the hair on his skin prickled to attention. Dammit. Even a year after their spilt she still had the power to affect him despite his best efforts to deny their chemistry.

"Lonely, I think," he answered. When she moved further into the room, every bit of him tuned into her. It was as if his body was hot-wired to hers, and it drove him crazy. The scent of sage wafted around them in a thin haze of heat. Or was the heat Callie? He cracked his knuckles and tried to come up with a reason to drop to the floor and army crawl out of there without looking into her face, but nothing came to mind.

Tension gripped his shoulders with every passing second, sinking in deep and holding tight.

"I know you don't want to be here, Dax. Let's just get through this and then we can go back to ignoring one another."

It was all too simple, but if it made his sister happy, he'd pretend for the next few hours that they were all friends again — pretend that he hadn't fucked up the best thing that had ever happened to him. And all because his damn jealousy got the best of him. He scrubbed a hand through his hair and sucked in the breath that

would have to suffice while he met Callie face on.
And damn it all to hell if she didn't look…
 Breathtaking.
 Dammit.

THREE

IF DAPHNE'S EYES were sapphire, then Dax's were thunderstorm blue. And all that stormy power warred behind thick, dark lashes and assaulted her better judgment.

In the year since she'd last laid eyes on him, he'd gained even more of an edge than he typically wore. His hair was untrimmed and hung dark around his eyes, a new scar lived on his left cheekbone, and she would swear — under oath — that his leather jacket fit tighter around his defined shoulders. Yeah, she might still have a bad case of the Daxs. Her grams had warned her from the very first time she'd climbed on the back of one of his bikes that a case of the Daxs would likely be incurable. But did she listen? No. That would have been far too easy. And if there was a hard way to do something, Callie took that route.

Standing in the same room as her former flame was near torture. The kind of torture that would bring the most hardened of criminals to their knees and make death seem like a freakin' picnic. Yeah, fun times.

"How did she get *you* here, Opie?"

His voice snaked over her skin, plucking her nerves like the strings on a tightly wound guitar. "The usual way," she replied as she tried to dodge his heated look, worried it might be potent enough to set the tips of her hair on fire.

"So, she just asked?"

His low chuckle washed over her with the ease of molten lava. A laugh of her own escaped beneath her slowly wilting facade of normalcy. "Pretty much. You?"

"Same." A crooked smile tugged at the corner of his mouth and completely undid her.

Before she actually turned into a puddle of mush, she took a breath, squared her shoulders, and rebuilt a smidgen of her resolve. "Look, I'll stay down here and find stuff to keep me busy. You can go up and work with Nic."

"You don't have to avoid us." Low, seductive, dark. All the things Dax represented wrapped up into one six-word phrase.

A lump fought for prime real estate somewhere between her stomach and throat while her brain raced faster than a derby winning horse. "I don't want to cause any more problems."

He reached out and tucked a stray curl behind her ear, leaving her resolve in shambles while her heart leapt in her chest.

"We're brothers. It's water under the bridge. Plus, I got this reminder to keep me from pissing him off in the future." He pointed to the scar on his cheek.

"Shit, Dax. What were you thinking?" A wave of guilt crashed over her in the perfect storm of what loving him was. Heat, guilt, fear, ecstasy — all rolled into one six foot-three inch package that could make any Victoria's Secret cover model blush when he stared at them with *that* look. The look that right now stripped her bare.

"That he had moved in on my girl."

She shook her head and begged her brain to work. "You're insane. You do know that, right?"

"That's what he told me." His eyes never moved. Instead, they dug deeper into her soul, looking for Goddess only knew what.

"I'll bet," she muttered.

"Yeah, then he drove the point home with his fists." His hand rubbed absently at his face and the scar on his skin.

"I can't believe you fought," she whispered more to herself than to him.

"Fought is a strong word for what happened." He reached for her and tilted her chin so that her eyes couldn't leave his.

Her breath did the logical thing and lodged in her throat, right where she didn't need it. "What happened then?"

"More like accusations were voiced, fists flew, faces got in the way, and then we walked away brothers." He paused and gave her an odd look before he released his hold on her. "Didn't Nic tell you all this?"

She shifted under his scrutiny and grappled for the words that would keep his temper in check. The memory of Dax wrapped around that blond bimbo, Maureen, still haunted her. "Nic and I don't talk anymore. Something about your fragile ego." Yup. So much for keeping the peace. Before he could draw her into a confrontation she'd regret, she relit her sage until smoke billowed in graceful waves. Callie waved the smoking sage between them in the worst smudging she'd ever done, turned heel, and ran for the modernized kitchen in the rear of the converted house.

17

As was her luck, she ran face-first into none other than the lighter version of Dax. Nic steadied her balance and gave her a smile that didn't reach his eyes. Unlike his brother, he was tall, lanky, and oh, wow, was that muscle under the fabric of his tee? Dammit. He was just as dreamy as the rest of the Barrens. Daphne was stunning. Dax was heartbreaking. And Nic? Nic was warm, solid, dependable, kind, trustworthy. All the things she should want in a man. And in some ways she did, but good gravy he was missing the one thing that made her pulse race when she looked his way. What it was he lacked, she couldn't say for sure, but it was enough to frustrate the crap outta her.

"Easy there, Cal. Where you going in such a hurry?"

"Away from me."

Dammit. This was Daphne's worst idea in the history of bad ideas. Callie backed out of Nic's grasp and glared at Dax over her shoulder.

"Where did you all disappear to?" Daphne asked, coming to Callie's rescue.

Callie handed Daphne the sage, ducked around the triplets, and wound her way back into the front room with the stained glass window. She gave it a good look and decided Dax was right. The man portrayed in the glass looked more lonely than sad. Almost like he was frozen in time, waiting for someone who never arrived. She inched closer to the window and studied him.

"I know why I look glum, but dude, who put a pickle in your lemonade?" She stared at the image and imagined a witty retort from the glass man. But like most things in reality, his silence was anticlimactic. From the foyer she heard the triplets grumbling like only siblings could. "Yeah, being lonely sucks," she whispered to the window-man.

A creak behind her was the only answer, but it set her nerves on edge. It was instinct that made her grab the pendant around her neck like a shield of some sort. It was silly, but deep down in some messed up part of her brain, she really believed that the darn thing was able to protect her from all the things that went bump in the night. Well, all the things that weren't Dax Barren, anyway.

She shook off the unease and turned, only to find herself face to chest with Dax. Dammit. She dropped her pendant to her chest and pushed past him to join Daphne and Nic on the converted third floor. He grabbed her hand, halting her movement up the stairs. In the beat that it took her to figure out what was happening, he had a hand threaded in her curls, and his breath tickled her lashes.

"Let's stop being lonely together."

Oh no he didn't.

"Just tonight."

He leaned closer so that his words vibrated along every oversensitive nerve in her skin.

Her nod was all it took. Lips met lips and heat flared, stirring what lay barely restrained beneath the surface. *Shit*. Her case of the Daxs was in full force.

FOUR

Something about Calliope kept Dax looking her way well into the evening. Whether it was her curses when the hammer missed a nail and landed on her fingers, the sweat that dripped down her brow in the most unladylike way, or the melodic tone of her laughter when plaster landed on her shoe. She was a siren and he a sailor lost at sea, her call too much of a temptation to resist. How easy it would be to lose himself in her warm embrace time and time again, repeating the mistakes of their youth.

By the time the last of the drywall was hung, he knew he couldn't go home without her, so he followed her out to her truck and opened the door for her like a good gentleman should. But instead of helping her into the cab, he pulled her into him and melted into the embrace. She smelled like strawberries and sage. Pure heaven. She fit in his arms like he remembered — soft and small against his broad hardness. One kiss was all it had taken to get her to agree earlier, so he went with his go-to noncommittal move and hoped for the best.

"Just tonight," he reiterated.

"Agreed. This doesn't mean we're back together."

"Mm-hmm," he murmured before his tongue found the sensitive flesh at the shell of her ear.

"I'm serious, Dax. Are you even listening to me?"

"Yeah. Just tonight," he echoed, releasing her. He studied her ass like a how-to book on bike engines as she climbed into the truck. "I'll follow you to the Dews," he said, adjusting the bulge in his jeans.

"Park around the corner. I don't want Grams getting the wrong idea."

"We'd hate that." A smile tugged at his lips.

He did as told and parked around the corner from the store. Even though the lights were still on inside, he headed straight to the back stairwell and climbed to the second floor apartment's exterior door. It was propped open and a trail of miscellaneous garments littered the floor in a trail that led to the bedroom. He closed the door behind him and added his jacket, boots, and jeans to the fabric breadcrumb trail. The shower sprang to life in the bathroom and directed him past the plush bed and gave him reason to shed his remaining layers.

He watched as hot water cascaded over Callie's body. The sight of her water-slicked curls turned his mouth drier than sandpaper. It had been too long since he'd indulged in such a luxury as a woman's softness and warmth. Since he'd seen Nic and Callie cozied up together in the intimate silence of lovers. The comfortable silence that he'd never been able to share with Callie. He was intense, there was no denying it, but that still didn't excuse her for going to his brother for the quiet she needed when he became "too much," as she'd claimed.

They both swore nothing had happened, but he couldn't wrap his brain around anyone being so close to the beauty that now sang in the shower, without their hands itching to touch her. And yet, here he was agreeing to only one night of her. One night of heat and passion. Then he'd walk away. For good this time. Because she'd never want him after tonight. The thought struck a chord and left him with a dull ache that was all too familiar. Regardless how difficult it was, he would find a way to leave her.

"Aren't you coming in?"

Everything that screamed at him to march his ass out of there landed with a thud shy of his reasoning center. It was the only reason that could explain his slipping behind the glass shower door to join her. Under the spray, he was transported back to a time when this was the norm. When she was his and life was simpler. When there wasn't a deal to be struck with the devil.

His heart sank when the realization struck. He wasn't here for her. Not even for himself. He was here to do the bidding of the being that held his family hostage for twenty-five long years. Hell, more than that if he counted all the way back to his grandfather. Guilt scorched over him, the flames of hell licking at his subconscious. But before the fire overtook him, Callie's hands began roaming. Slipping, sliding, caressing all of him — brushing away what haunted him.

Like the long-lost lovers they were, there were no awkward moments of over thinking or hesitancy. Instead, he braced himself on the shower wall and kissed her into a frenzied fever. His hands refused to stay off her body. He wrapped himself in her arms until he was mere inches away from sinking into her depths. Heaven awaited him, but she pushed back.

"Condom?"

"Shit."

She unwound her legs from his hips and slid to her feet. "Let's go into the bedroom."

"Since when do you want to use a bedroom?" Part of Callie's appeal had always been her uninhibited nature. And yet, here she was surprising him. She turned off the spray, stepped out, and handed him a towel. He watched as she dried herself then fingered the pendant strung around her neck.

Much as he hated to admit it, this was the easiest way to get his hands on what the devil needed, despite the unforgivable nature of what he was about to do. He slipped his hands over the skin at her neck, caressing, teasing, tempting with each stroke of his fingers. When a soft sigh slipped through her parted lips, he took the invitation and kissed her; kissed her for the moment, for the year he'd been without her, for the eternity he'd spend indebted to her.

"Take it off." If his voice shook, she didn't seem to notice, but his hands trembled when he plucked the chain off her skin.

"Whatever turns you on, big guy." She stilled as he worked the clasp.

"You turn me on. Always have. Since day one." He set the necklace on the nightstand, kissed the nape of her neck, and flopped onto the bed, dragging her down with him. "And lucky me, I get you all to myself."

"For tonight."

"Whatever. You're mine. Tonight." The twinkle in her eyes did more for his spirit than it should, but added a ton of guilty weight to his heart.

"Are you going to talk all night, or are you planning on doing me?"

She was wicked. The insatiable woman did funny things to his heart, and if he were anyone else in the world, he'd find a way to cherish her the way she deserved to be loved. Instead, he'd give her all that he could. He hated this piece of him that would satisfy all her wants and needs tonight and break her heart tomorrow. He shook the thought out of his mind and did what he did best — crawl between her legs and give her the ride of her life.

Before the pull of exhaustion lulled Dax into the safe embrace of sleep beside Callie, he slid the pendant into his pants pocket, dressed, and snuck out, closing the door behind him. Near his bike, he removed the pendant and examined it under the glow of a streetlamp. The stone was similar to the one in the pendant Daphne wore, but different — as if it was an artisan piece and not some cheap mass-produced piece of costume jewelry.

While the necklace was nice, it was old and probably not of much value. He contemplated why Callie would wear the piece. Daphne's was supposed to ward off evil and was supposedly handed down from some high and mighty witch. But for Callie to have a similar one? That struck him as odd. He tried to remember a time he hadn't seen her wearing it and couldn't come up with a single moment. Whatever it was that made this thing so special he couldn't feel it. It was only an old necklace.

One he hoped Callie wouldn't miss.

FIVE

THE HARSH RINGING of a telephone yanked Callie out of one crazy dream. She shook the image of a man calling for help behind a colored pane of glass out of her head and felt around for the phone on her nightstand.

"What?" Her tone was less than nice, but so was waking a girl up at, she blinked at the glowing numbers on her alarm clock, and swore. "Shit."

"Where the heck are you?"

"Daph?" She could hear the agitation in her friend's voice over the line, and when Daphne got agitated, look out below.

"I'm outside the shop and it's all locked up. You owe me an explanation."

What the hell was she talking about? It was five in the morning. "An explanation? For what?"

"Don't you dare act like my dumbass brother didn't follow you home last night. Is he still there? Is that why you didn't open the store yet?"

Callie propped herself on her elbow and yawned. A quick swat of her hand on the bed behind her confirmed what she already knew was true. Dax wasn't there. He'd kept to his word and was gone in time for the new day to dawn. Before she could reassure her friend, she heard the familiar jingle of keys in the apartment's lock.

"Are you letting yourself into my place?" The nerve!

"Are you both *decent*?" The words sing-songed through the receiver and the hallway.

"Dammit Daphne," Callie yelled and sprang out of bed. Thankfully she had the good sense to put pajamas on last night before curling up beside Dax. She let the phone drop and dangle on its cord. "What in the actual hell are you thinking right now?" She stormed through the bedroom and right up to within a breath's distance from stepping on her friend's toes. "It's none of your damn business what your brother and I did, or didn't do, last night. And in case you're wondering, there was a lot of doing."

"Oh gross. I don't want to hear that. I thought…" She paused. "Do you have sex hair? Oh shit. You *do* have sex hair."

"You thought wrong," Callie interrupted. It was bad enough Daphne woke her on her only day off, but then to just stomp in here throwing all sorts of accusations and innuendoes around, Callie was going to head her off at the pass.

"Your brother and I are adults, so drop it. As for opening the store, Grams is working this morning, and I was planning on sleeping in."

"You're right. It's none of my business what you and Dax do." Daphne turned around and went straight for the coffee press that lived on the kitchen counter. "It *was* Dax, right?"

Callie grabbed a pillow off the nearest end of the couch and chucked it at her friend. It hit Daphne square in the back with a satisfying thud.

"Hey," Daphne whined. She plucked the pillow off the floor and tossed it on the couch.

"You deserved it," Callie challenged. She grabbed the coffee press from her friend's hands and smiled. "Let's do the machine today. I need coffee faster than the press this morning. Someone woke me up from a very satisfying night's sleep."

"I'm sorry. Is that what you want to hear?"

"Well, that's a start." Callie scooped coffee beans into the grinder and gave them a whirl. When they were perfectly ground, she poured them into the automatic coffee maker and added water. Soon the aroma of the gods wafted through the kitchen. She grabbed her favorite oversized mug from the dish drainer and another for Daphne from the cabinet. "So what really has you here this early on a Sunday morning?"

Confusion creased Daphne's brow. "Is it only Sunday? Oh. Well, that explains a lot." She ran a hand through her sleep-tussled hair.

Callie studied her friend. In all the years they'd known each other, she wasn't sure she had ever seen her friend so out of sorts. Her hair looked unwashed and hung in tangles around her face. And were those the same clothes that she had been wearing last night when they finished the drywall? "What's wrong, Daph?" Callie watched as her friend carefully flopped onto the sofa with her coffee. Were those dark circles under her eyes?

"You're going to think I'm insane, and maybe I am."

Callie folded herself into an overstuffed easy chair, sipped her coffee, and considered her reply. Finally she went for friend and not smart-ass. "We both know you aren't insane. Tell me what happened."

"Remember the other day when I told you I thought that maybe there was someone in the house?" She took a tentative sip from her mug.

"Yeah. Mirror streaks and sliding covers." Callie motioned for her friend to continue.

"Well, last night after everyone left, I fell asleep in the drawing room on the chaise."

Callie watched Daphne's hands tremble and was confused by the expectant look on her tired face. "Okay? So, you fell asleep."

Daphne cut her off before she could get another word out.

"Not okay. Because I woke up and I swear someone kissed me."

"Are you sure it wasn't one of your brothers giving you a peck on the cheek or something?"

"I'm positive, and the kiss wasn't on my cheek."

Daphne's words sank in and spiked every hair on Callie's arms. "So what are you saying? Someone broke into the B&B and made out with you?"

"No. I think the Victorian is haunted."

Callie stared at her friend. "I think you've read too many of the Belvidere Historical Society's pamphlets, my friend. There aren't ghosts. And your new place isn't haunted. I think it's just big and you're all alone, and well, you have every reason to be paranoid, all things considered." The memory of almost losing her friend to the devil years ago was never far from the front of her mind. "Plus, I know your birthday is coming up and it'll be thirteen years since the last time that monster came looking for you. Maybe it's just your imagination."

"I'm not imagining it. Can you come over and bring one of your spell books or something? Heck, doesn't Grams have an old Ouija board or something?" She set her mug on the antique coffee table and twirled a piece of hair around her finger. "*Please*, Cal? I think I'm losing my mind."

"You know I'm not going to let you live in a place that's freaking you out. Let me get dressed and we'll head over."

SIX

"SHIT." CALLIE'S NECK felt naked as she bounced down the road in her truck toward the B&B. Last night it had seemed out of character for Dax to request that she remove the necklace, but in the heat of the moment, rational thought had flown the coop. She fingered the hollow of her throat and made a mental note to find it and return it to its rightful place around her neck as soon as she got home.

Callie grabbed the board game, a bag full of spell books, and followed her friend into the Victorian. Unlike every other time she had entered the house, heaviness landed on her the minute she crossed the threshold. Her feet froze just within the doorway, blood pounded in her ears, and whispers skated along every nerve ending. She jumped back through the doorway and dropped everything, her arms unable to function as designed any longer.

"Psst. Lady, you look like you've seen a ghost." A male voice taunted from beside her.

Fast enough to get whip lash, she turned to find the source of the voice. Nothing. Now maybe she was the one losing her mind.

"Hey, did you hear me?" The same voice called again.

"Who's there? And why are you trying to scare the shit outta me?" She swept her gaze over the shadows that lurked under the huge covered porch where it wrapped around to the side of the house. Her feet rebelled her brain's demand to move, until the voice sounded again.

"You can hear me? Hot damn! I'm over here."

Her heartbeat kicked up a notch and enough adrenaline flooded her system to get even the oldest of engines into motion. She raced to the corner of the porch, rounded it, and stopped dead in her tracks. From the corner of her eye she caught movement in the window. A closer look only made things worse. She rubbed her eyes and sent a silent prayer into the heavens that, if she was having a stroke, it passed quick and when someone found her body they'd make sure she didn't die with her hair looking as bad as Daphne's.

"Hey. What's wrong with you?" The male voice crooned from the thick colored panes.

"What's wrong with me?" she hissed, looking from side to side to make sure there were no witnesses to her steady decline into insanity. "What do you think? I'm standing here talking to a man in the window." She bent nearer to the stained glass visage and lowered her voice further. "I'm dying, right? That's what's happening right now, some out of body experience?"

"Lady, you're as close to dying as I am."

And then her life got a whole lot weirder. The man made of colored glass shapes moved, and not just a little, either. He patted himself down as if

31

checking to make sure he was still real, whole, and alive.

"Oh, *hell* no. This can't be happening to me." Callie pinched the skin on her left forearm with her right hand until she was sure she'd have a bruise. "Damn it." She rubbed the area to soothe the hurt she had inflicted.

"Who told you to pinch yourself?" The glass man threw his hands up in the air. Well, as much as he could, considering he was trapped within the confines of the colored panes. "So, are you going to help me or not?"

"Help you? How?"

"Well, I've been trapped in this damn window for a long time. And if I'm not mistaken, you're a witch."

"A witch? Who told you that? I mean, what would make you think that?" Heat raced up her chest and warmed her face.

"Oh, please. The only way you would be able to hear me would be if you were on the magical spectrum. I've been waiting for a long time for someone to come along that would be able to free me."

"Wait a second. I'm a non-practicing witch. I don't have any powers or anything. I can make herbal remedies and stuff, but that's all. So the fact that I'm talking to you is insane. You do realize that, right?"

"If you're insane, then how come you can hear me right now?"

"Who says I can?" Callie shook her head and glanced over her shoulder and muttered, "Callie, you are losing your ever-loving mind. You need more sleep."

"Your name is Callie? Mine is Jason. Jason Clark."

"Cal, where'd you go?" Daphne's voice carried from the front door.

"Shit! That's Daphne. Shush."

"She can't hear me. I've been trying to get her attention since the first time she looked at this old haunt." A glassy grating laugh followed.

"Over here, Daph," she called. She glared at the man in the windowpane. "Just stay quiet."

"Whatever, it won't make a difference either way," he argued.

"Hey, what happened? I thought you were following me."

"Yeah. I thought I heard something over here." She glared at Jason. "Sounded like a cat in heat or something." That shut him up, but he flipped her the bird in retaliation. Callie threw her hand over his glass one to conceal the gesture, but realized that upon closer inspection, he was seated just as he had been yesterday; the same sad and lonely look in his eyes.

"Are you okay?"

Puzzled, Callie moved closer to the window and witnessed a smirk coupled with an exaggerated wink. She swung around. "Did you just see that?"

"See what?" Daphne asked at the same time that Jason proclaimed, "She can't see anything. Only you can."

"The man in the window. He moved." Callie pointed at Jason.

"No, he didn't. Are you sure you're okay? You look like you've seen a ghost."

"She saw a ghost, but she doesn't believe me," he chimed in.

"I think you're right about the house, Daph. Something is off." She looked back at the window. If she was losing her mind, she wasn't about to admit it. Instead, she linked arms with her friend and went back to the front of the house.

"Don't leave me in here. Come on, you can't just leave me here like this," he hollered.

I'm pretty sure you're a work of my imagination, so I sure can leave you right there in the window, raced through her head as she turned away.

"Wait. Stop!"

Callie flipped Jason the bird behind Daphne's back and followed her back into the house.

SEVEN

BEING SUMMONED WAS worse than waiting in a damn forest. Drammelech contemplated what reason the mortal would have for calling him this early in the morning. Although he was a devil, he still needed to sleep, but explaining that to humans ruined the illusion. He wore the fear-mongering, all-powerful, take no prisoners persona like a second skin.

"I have your pendant."

Had the man added "dark one" then the image would've been worth the wake-up summons. "So your sister handed it over?" His black heart leapt in his chest.

"No. I was able to find another."

"Interesting."

"Not as interesting as you think." The man kicked his boot into the dirt. It was becoming a habit that gave so much insight into the man's mental state.

"The only people to wear the pendants were two long-dead witches." He studied the man's face and debated the authenticity of the item hanging between his long fingers.

"It matches the one Daphne wears. It's got to be a second pendant."

"Doubtful. I have an idea where the other one is."

"Look, demon, you asked for it, and I delivered. You owe me a conversation with my mother." He thrust the talisman into the devil's waiting hands.

The second it touched Drammelech's skin, smoke wafted into the air. The metal heated in his hand, glowed red, and began to warp. The piece of quartz nestled amid the ebbing metal slipped from it's embrace and fell to the ground. He dropped the heated metal and gingerly picked up the stone from the ground. The power encased within sprang forth as if it had a life of its own. Warm, feminine, old. *Delila*. His mother's name sliced through his mind on a shiver of pain. It was a genuine article — he could feel it the longer he held it in his palm.

The old magic swirled around him, bubbling into something bigger than himself — bigger than what his mother had been. Life changing.

"Now where's my mother?" the man demanded.

"She's right here." Drammelech waved his hand and revealed the visage of Hope Barren.

"Mom." The man's mouth gaped at the woman before him.

"What did you do, Dax?" Her eyes went wide, but a wave of Drammelech's hand muted any further words.

"I did what I had to so you can come home to us."

Still a little boy at heart that missed his mommy, the man's face crumbled and tears glistened in his eyes. Under different circumstances, to a different audience it would be heartwarming, but

Drammelech's heart was stone cold and nothing shy of a miracle could make it waver.

"Oh, this won't allow her to leave. Thisssss is so you can speak with her and I can finally break the spell that holds me here."

"No. You said if I brought it, I could see her."

"I've kept my word," the devil added then gestured with a sweep of his hand until Hope dissolved from human view.

"Bring her back."

"Until your sister joins me, your mother stays put."

"But you have the necklace. Why do you still need Daphne?"

"That is none of your concern. But I suggest you have a little talk with your sister and let her know that I'll be coming for her. *Soon.*"

"She will never willingly join you." Venom dripped from every word Dax uttered.

"Ah, but now that I have this…" Drammelech pulled the stone from his pocket, "she will not be able to hide from me." With one last sweeping gesture, he dissolved from view.

EIGHT

CALLIE SPENT THE greater part of her morning side-stepping the multitude of ghosts lurking about in each and every room in the Victorian. By the time Daphne begged to put the Ouija board to use, Callie was done.

"We can't bring that out. Not now."

"Why not? If there's something here, I need to find a way to communicate with it and tell it to leave." Her friend paced the front room while Jason waved frantically from the glass pane behind her. "You know I have a soft open in a couple of weeks, and I can't have people staying in a haunted B&B."

"Oh? Why not? A hotel with haunts? It could start a new trend," Callie offered as she avoided another ghostly person.

"Something like that will bring you tons of business," Jason chimed in from his window.

Callie waved him off when Daphne turned her back for a moment. A swipe of her finger across her throat got the message across. Sure, it stank of mob boss, but it worked. Jason stopped dancing around in the glass like a cartoon character on crack.

"Hotel for haunts. Yeah, right," Daphne muttered. "I can't afford to lose business before I can get this off the ground. Strange happenings could ruin me."

Callie froze as an old woman swayed by dancing to music only she could hear. "Well, I'm pretty sure you need to rethink that."

"What? Why?" Daphne shot her a puzzled look.

"Do you want the good news or the bad news first?" Callie danced around the twirling ghost and leaned against Jason's window; the ghost she knew was better than accidentally bumping into a strange one. Goodness, what had happened to her life that a ghost trapped in a window was now deemed "safe?"

"There's bad news?"

"Yeah. More of it than good, I'm afraid."

"Hit me with it. All of it."

Callie watched as her oldest friend straightened to her full height and squared her shoulders, ready to deal with the news she was about to deliver. It sucked having to be the one to tell her friend that her dream was more dead than alive.

"The house is teeming with spirits. A whole bunch just sit there and don't do too much, some are downright talkative, and lets not forget twirling Sue over there." She gestured to the middle of the room where the spirit twirled and danced.

"Sue?"

"I don't know her real name, but she was freaking me out and I needed to call her something."

Daphne froze. "Where is she now?"

Callie watched as the ghost spun again, this time drifting right through Daphne. Yeah, there was no way in hell she was about to tell her friend that a ghost had just violated her. "She's over that aways." Callie pointed off to her friend's left. "Can't you feel her?"

"No. Can you?"

"Not exactly, but I can sure as heck see her." Callie rubbed her tired eyes and shook her head.

"I thought you smudged yesterday?"

"I did. And yesterday I didn't see any of this."

"Then how come you can see them now?"

"I honestly don't know, but I'm not gonna lie, it's freaking me out." An involuntary shiver ran up her spine. "Let's go back to the shop. I'll ask Grams if she can help get rid of your poltergeist problem, and then I'm gonna take another shower." She shivered again as another ghost popped out of the woodwork beside her and ran right through the left side of her body as if she didn't exist.

Dammit. Now she had ghost goo on her.

Callie rolled through almost every stop sign between the B&B and the Dews in her hurry. She had wanted Daphne to come with her, but she had refused with the excuse of still wanting to get some finishing touches done on her master suite.

The wind chimes on the front door of the Dews jangled as she breezed through and went straight to the gourmet coffee system.

"What's got you all hot under the collar this morning?" Grams asked.

"I think I'm losing my mind," she answered and leaned over to place a peck of a kiss on her grandmother's cheek. "That old Victorian that Daphne's converting?" She trailed off in search of the right words, but finding none, she powered on. "It's haunted. Like seriously haunted. Everywhere I look there's some discarded soul." She reached down into the cabinet beneath the counter for her favorite mug, only to find the spirit of a young woman curled in a ball over in the corner.

"Shit! They're here too."

Her grandmother grabbed her by the shoulders and held her tight, forcing her to meet her gaze. "What's here?"

Callie turned her head back to the young woman cowered in the corner behind the counter. "A woman. Young, maybe mid-twenties. Straight hair. Blond maybe. I don't know. Why?"

Grams pulled down the neck of Callie's blouse and stepped back. "Where's your necklace?"

"I don't know. Upstairs somewhere, I think." Subconsciously she touched the place it usually hung nestled on her collarbone.

"Go get it." Grams gestured to the private entrance in the rear of the store. "Now."

A last glance at the woman revealed more than Callie was ready to see. The woman who had previously been curled into a cocoon on the floor now stood, curious eyes focused on her. A look, familiar yet alien, etched itself on the woman's face. Callie slid past her and ran to the apartment.

Once inside her bedroom, she stood rooted to the floor as she played the mental game of where she saw it last. Her eyes kept returning to the bedside table but it was empty. No pendant, no nothing. She checked the floor, the covers, even behind the bed, but the necklace was nowhere to be found. She turned toward the bathroom to see if she had left it on the counter instead and ran right through the ghost from downstairs. Gooseflesh pebbled her skin while every hair on her arms sprang to life like a standing ovation at the end of a Broadway show.

"Why are you here?" She didn't actually expect the ghost to answer, but understanding dawned on its translucent face.

"Calliope Jane, can you really see me?"

Callie reared back until her legs met the bed and she toppled onto the pillow-topped mattress. She rolled, sprang up on all fours, and stared the ghost in the eyes. The silence carried through as the two sat poised on the precipice of something larger than life: the realization that Callie was face to face with the mother she had lost so many years ago.

"Oh my gosh. It's really you, isn't it?" She tilted her face and moved to the edge of the bed to take a closer look. "How are you here right now?"

"Callie-pie, I've always been right here. Ever since the day I died."

"Then why is it I'm just now seeing you? Besides, isn't there an afterlife or something that you're supposed to be enjoying?"

"Not exactly." Her mother looked upward as if looking for the words to explain herself. "There's something wrong with the natural order of things. Like there's a lock on the gates between the planes. There's a lot of restless souls here. Souls waiting to move on."

"That explains the Victorian overflowing with ghosts, but still doesn't explain why I'm seeing them for the first time now."

The silhouette of her mother wavered as if being tossed about in the wind. "You took off your necklace. Don't you remember me telling you to wear it always?"

"Yeah, but…" Callie trailed off.

"Oh, I know about your visitor last night, Calliope Jane."

A rush of heat washed over her face and left a bright blush in its wake. "Mom," she hissed, "You shouldn't be watching *that*."

"Oh, I assure you I didn't. But you should know I saw your visitor leave with the chain of your necklace waving from his pocket."

"No. Dax would never..." She stopped mid-thought. Why was she defending him? He had a history of doing things she never thought he'd do — why would this be any different? "Did you happen to see where he took it?"

"If I tell you, will you promise not to do anything about it?"

"Sure." She shrugged. Lying to her mother wasn't as hard as she might've thought it'd be. Maybe it had something to do with her being dead for most of Callie's life.

"He took it to Elech. The restless spirits are all talking about it. And now that that monster has it, everything wandering this plane is out of sorts." Her mother looked around as if there was a chance the monster she spoke of might be lurking in the corners. "It's chaos. If he has a pendant, it means he can access our magic."

"What magic? And who's Elech?"

"The magic all Dewsberry women are born with. And Elech is the devil that killed me years ago when I took off my pendant. His mother was an ancestor of ours, his father was the Devil, and we are his link to getting what he needs. His mom wrote it all out it in her journals. Didn't Grams tell you?"

"Like the devil, devil?" Of everything her mom had said, the idea of the devil having children stuck in her mind the most. Good gracious, what woman in her right mind would sleep with the devil? If he was anything like his son, he was pure evil. The memory of Daphne's near abduction lived too close to the surface to ignore.

And of course it figured that one of Callie's ancestors would be the *one* woman in all of history to sleep with the devil. It was no secret that Dewsberry woman weren't known for having the best taste in men — her Grams being the exception to the rule.

Her mother nodded. "His mother locked him here on this plane for the entirety of his existence and created the pendants to protect her remaining daughters. Unfortunately, now that he has one, you and Grams are at risk."

"Oh shit. That means Daphne is too."

"Who's Daphne?" Confusion creased her mother's ghostly features.

"A friend that Thirteen, I mean Elech, tried to kidnap years ago. Grams gave her a pendant to protect her, but if it won't work because he has one, she's in trouble." Callie dodged her mother as she ducked back down into the shop.

"Grams, where are the old journals that you never hide well?" She yelled as she rifled through the back section of the store where she remembered last finding the old leather-bound tomes.

Her grandmother rounded the shelves, "What in tarnation are you yelling about?"

"The old journals. The ones with the spells in them."

"Callie Jane, if I've told you once, I've told you a million times that you should keep your nose out of those."

The scolding was one she was familiar with, but she ignored it and kept pawing through the dusty books.

"I think I saw her put them in the back of the historical witchcraft section," her mom piped up, blinking into existence behind her and sending a fresh chill down her spine.

"Don't do that. You scared me."

"I'm just trying to help." A sheepish look graced her mother's frozen-in-time face.

"Who are you talking to? Are you feeling all right?" Grams turned the corner and reached an arm for her forehead, but Callie ducked and spun around to the historical witchcraft section.

Her mother pointed a ghostly finger toward the far corner of the bookcase. Callie snagged a stool and reached up on her tippy toes to pull books off the indicated shelf. True to her word, the ribbon secured leather-bound journals were tucked back behind the other books. She slid them to the edge and turned to her grandmother. "Can you get me a bag for these?"

Her face ashen, Grams asked, "How'd you find them?"

"Not now, Grams. I have to get over to Daphne's. I think the monster who tried to take her when we were kids is coming for her."

"That's nonsense. Her mother and I made sure she'd be safe."

"Yeah, but that was before my pendant went missing."

"It's missing?"

"Yeah, and Mom heard that Dax handed it over to the fucking devil, so I've got to get over there and find something in one of these," she gestured to the stack of journals, "to help her."

"Your mother? Calliope, what are you talking about?"

"Here's the quick version. I can see ghosts without the pendant. Turns out Mom's been hanging around the Dews since she died. But if Mom's right about these journals, the devil's mom was the witch that wrote these. Our ancestor. We can't leave Daphne all alone to defend herself against the thing that took Hope's soul."

"Let me get a few things and I'll come with you." Her grandmother busied herself with selecting a few other books and then rummaged through a display full of crystals. She selected a few and pocketed them.

"What about the store?"

"The most important things in this place are coming with us." She opened a satchel for Callie to drop the journals into. "Let's go."

"Wait for me," her mother said drifting behind them.

Yeah, this was going to be the weirdest party ever. A ghost and a witch going to war against a devil to save someone's soul.

In other words, just another Sunday.

NINE

WHEN CALLIE PULLED alongside the Victorian, her eyes immediately sought out the stained glass window that was home to Jason. Her mother had chatted nearly the entire way over in the car while Callie played translator for Grams. She spared a quick glance at her grandmother, realization dawning. Communicating with her dead mother was a lot for her grandmother to take in. Maybe it was something Callie should have kept to herself, but at the time it hadn't crossed her mind.

They hopped down from the cab of her truck while her mom went right through the back door of the king cab.

"I would've opened the door for you," Callie said to her ghostly mom as she led the way to the front door.

"I'm perfectly capable of opening my own door," Grams answered before understanding crossed her face. "You weren't talking to me, were you?"

"Nope. Mom oozed through the door."

"I'm not sure I'll ever get used to this," Grams said under her breath.

"You know, if you took off your pendant, I bet you'd see her too."

"I wouldn't dare. Taking that pendant off was how your mother died. I'm not ready to be dead. I still have more life in me than the silly bunny that bangs on a drum in the commercials."

"Hey, you're back! Are you finally gonna get me outta this damn window?" Jason called from his spot round the corner of the house.

Callie shook her head and knocked on the glass-paneled front door.

"Aw, come on. Do you want me to beg? I'll beg if that's what it'll take to get out of here." He prattled on and on while she waited for Daphne to open the door.

Finally, she'd had enough.

"Look, who's to say you even deserve to be let out of that window? For all I know, you were put there for a perfectly reasonable reason." She marched around the porch and cut him a dark look just as she heard the front door open. Callie turned away from Jason and almost knocked into her grandmother who stood right beside her, staring, mouth agape.

"Grams, I'm so glad you came to help." Daphne edged around the corner of the house and threw her arms around the older woman. Since her own mom had become unreachable, Daphne had gotten close to Callie's grandmother.

"Come inside. Let me show you around." Daphne released Grams and held the door wide for them. "Did Callie tell you it's haunted?"

"She did," Grams answered as she followed Daphne into the grand foyer.

Callie skipped the tour and headed straight to the drawing room and Jason's window.

"You know, I'm stuck here because some dame decided she didn't like the idea of me dating someone besides her. She was crazy," Jason explained. "One day we were having breakfast on a bearskin rug in front of a roaring fire, and the next minute I was trapped in here. At least she had the forethought to put me back in my clothes before she locked me in here."

"He sounds a little off his rocker," her mom chimed in, scaring Callie almost out of her skin.

"Mom! You can't keep popping up like that! I thought you were following Grams and Daph around."

"Why? I have waited for so long to talk to you and I'm not ready to give it up." She gestured with a hand to the window. "Who's that, Callie-pie?"

"Callie-pie?" Jason laughed so hard he nearly tumbled onto the stained green shards that looked like grass.

"Knock it off, glass boy." Callie rolled her eyes and turned back to her mom's pulsating visage. "He's just one of the many ghosts hanging around here. Although, I don't understand why he's in the windowpane while the others just mill around." As if Callie's words had conjured her, dancing Sue waltzed into the room and took a spin around. Her dance halted and she stopped dead when she bumped into Callie's mom.

"Who are you? You shouldn't be here," the ghostly woman accused. Her face contorted as if she was narrowing her empty eyes at Callie's mom. She turned her eyes on Callie. "She shouldn't be here," she reiterated. "She will be stuck here with us now."

Callie's heart jumped and her nerve endings prickled to attention. "What are you talking about?"

"The witch's curse. She'll be stuck here with us now. Any soul that enters, stays." The ghost shook her head, shrugged her apparition shoulders, and retreated muttering under her lack of breath.

"What was that about?"

Callie shrugged and turned back to Jason. "Do you know anything about what she said?"

"Of course I do. Why do you think I've been asking you to help me get the hell outta here? That crazy witch cursed me to this window and everyone else in here. I told you she was nuts."

"But my mom didn't die here," Callie argued. "Try the door, mom."

She watched as her mom tried to morph through the wall out to the porch and bounced back like a snapping rubber band.

"It's not gonna work. Not everyone here died here. Some were loved ones who came to visit and got stuck," Jason announced, a solemn look on his face.

"How do we get her unstuck?" Panic colored her tone. After twenty years of not having her mom around, Callie wasn't ready to let her go just because of some damned spell.

"If I knew how to get unstuck, do you really think I'd still be in here talking to you? I mean, you're cute and all, but I've been here for a long time."

Dread sunk like a lead balloon in her stomach. "How long?" She swallowed against the rising bile in her throat.

"Let's see. I was born in 1925. Met Teresa in 1946. She cursed me later that year, I think. What year is it again?"

Callie did some mental math. "Sixty-nine years."

Jason let out a low whistle. "Seems longer, but if you say so."

Callie stumbled away from the window and flopped into a chaise nearby. The worry etched on her mother's ghostly face stung. Her mind raced as snippets of thoughts swirled around not making a full connection. Jason had been here for almost seventy years and now her mom was stuck.

"You're a witch. That means you can fix this. Right?"

Callie stared straight into Jason's glass eyes. "What gives you the idea that *I* can fix this? I'm still not convinced that I haven't lost my freaking mind." She got up too fast, her vision blurring, and whirled around when the sound of Daphne and Grams coming hit her ears.

"What happened, Cal? You look like you've seen a ghost," teased Daphne.

"Not funny." She shook her head and pointed at Jason in the window. "Can either of you see him?"

"Sure I can see him, honey," Grams confirmed. The crease between her brows went from its usual thin line into a full-on canyon in the middle of her forehead.

Callie turned back to Jason, who was doing some ridiculous hip gyrating move while waving his arms above his head lasso style. Laughter ripped from her gut, torn straight from the core of her, putting the world right for the first time since she'd heard him earlier that morning.

Hands squeezed her shoulders and the smell of her grandmother's vanilla perfume wafted over her. "I'm going to guess that you aren't seeing a sad young man sitting on a tree stump," Grams said.

"Not even remotely close." She watched as Jason did a gallop move.

"So this happened when you lost your necklace?" Daphne fingered the pendant hung at her collarbone.

"I didn't lose it. Dax stole it."

Daphne and Grams both had the same look of shock mixed with disbelief on their faces. Neither spoke even though their mouths moved in tandem wordlessness. Daphne was the first to recover, but Callie never dreamed her next move would be to reach behind herself and unclip her own pendant. She refastened the clasps and set it on top of an old upright piano. She moved closer to Jason's window, eyes in a full-on squint.

"I still don't see anything. What do you see?"

Callie turned back to the window and Jason's goofy face: eyes crossed, tongue out, thumb firmly planted on his nose as his fingers wiggled in the glass. "I'm not sure I can explain just how much of a dork he's being right now." She turned her back on Jason in time for Grams to begin struggling with the clasp on her pendant. "What are you doing?"

"I miss my daughter."

If there was ever an answer that Callie couldn't argue with it was that. She nodded and went to help with the hook. As soon as the pendant left her grandmother's neck and was fully in Callie's hands, Jason appeared back to his seated position on the stump in the field of grassy glass and the ghosts in the room disappeared. Grams turned, scanning the room with laser focus.

"I don't see her." She turned to Callie, worry created new wrinkles on her skin. "Where is she?"

Callie shrugged. She squinted at Jason's window and waited for him to say something, but he sat still, quiet. It must be the pendant in her hand. She crossed the room and laid the necklace on the window sill beneath Jason's pane of colored glass. The moment her skin lost contact with the jewelry, her mother blinked into existence right in front of her face.

A startled yelp squeaked from her lips. "I found her, Grams." She stepped away from her mother and pointed with her index finger, just shy of actually permeating her mother's ghostly form.

"I don't see her." Tears welled in her grandmother's eyes. It had to be awful to know that your child was so close but still so far away.

"There has to be something you can do, Grams." Callie struggled to find a reasonable explanation for her ability to see the deceased, while her Grams couldn't. "You know, I didn't see her right away. Maybe it'll just take some time."

"Look, I know you're all having a moment, but I thought you were going to get me outta here."

Callie whirled on Jason's windowpane and wagged a finger at him. "Don't you start with me or I'll leave your ass in there."

"You promised."

She flipped him the bird and turned back to her grandmother. Daphne had her arms wrapped around the older woman while tears freely flowed. As touching as the scene was on its own, it was more so when both her mother and three other ghosts all surrounded the two women with bowed heads. If there were a camera that could capture that image, it would break hearts the world over.

"She's with you, Grams, even if you can't see her, she's there."

"Well, well. What do we have here?"

Callie froze as fear washed through her like a tsunami wave. Everyone in the room, ghosts included, paled as the gravely voice of the devil raked over their nerve endings.

"So it's true. This little stone is all that was keeping me from ending all of you."

Grams shoved Daphne behind her and faced the evil that stood before them. "You aren't welcome here, Drammelech."

The bravado that coated every syllable was merely for show, Callie knew it for a fact in her heart, but still, Grams impressed her. As it was, Callie was shaking in her flip-flops.

Daphne slowly moved to Callie's side and grabbed her hand. "We need to do something." Her whispered words danced with panic and fear. "We can't let him hurt anyone else."

Callie squeezed her friend's hand and let every conscious thought in her mind meld together until the most minuscule of plans began to form in the back corner of her brain. As a child, she remembered a song — a verse at most. A woman had sung it to her night after night, over and over again, until sleep would steal the woman away, and now, in the back of her mind it wormed its way to the surface.

Callie's voice, low and seductive, full of warmth and promise broke the silence in the house. Thirteen's eyes left Grams and turned on her, the weight of his stare enough to almost make her lose her pitch, but she powered through. Power sizzled through the air, growing, undulating, and churning into something tangible; something Callie could feel wrapping around her heart as she continued the chorus. She fed off the energy as it overtook her, streaming in and threatening to burst forth like a missile locked and loaded mid-battle.

Behind her, the glass of the window rattled against its lead bonds as if the magic flowing through her first passed through it, until in an explosion of brilliant colors and razor-sharp shards, the window exploded. Yet, every sliver of cut glass shot through the air perfectly aimed toward the monster in the room.

Thirteen raised his arms to shield his face and fled as the bite of the broken bits sank into his skin.

"What did you do?" Jason's voice rang clear by her ear. Callie whirled around and came face to chest with a living, breathing man. He quirked an eyebrow and smiled a half smile. Behind him, Callie watched as her mom's spectral form flew through the wall that before had held her captive. Was the spell broken?

"Callie?" Jason offered a small wave then awkwardly stuck his hand out toward her. "Nice to meet you in the flesh."

Callie's tongue stuck to the dry roof of her mouth as she gaped at the man. His hair wasn't as dark as she had assumed now that sunlight played on the silken strands, and eyes she had assumed were brown were ringed with gold and held the sparkle of green flecks. His chest was much broader than the glass panes made it appear and tapered down to hips solid enough to hold her if she leapt into his arms and wrapped her long legs around them. Heat raced to her face as the mental image of being in Jason's arms tangled with the hormones shooting through her bloodstream.

Shit.

He was *fine*. The kind of fine that took her breath away and made her wish she was his type; regardless of what his type was. And there he stood, still waiting for her to shake his damn hand like they were just meeting for the first time.

"Calliope?" Her grandmother's voice shook.

"Callie!" Daphne's high pitched shriek was enough to pull her eyes away from Jason and face her best friend, but the danger that she had thought was past, stood solidly behind her grandmother with a sharp dagger at her throat.

Adrenaline spiked her bloodstream, sending her into the fight abyss.

"Let. Her. Go." Her voice never wavered, her tone never changed. Thirteen held her grandmother's life in his hands and with a twitch of the blade it would be over in an instant.

Daphne's hand still clutched Grams' despite the devil's close proximity.

The weight of a hand on her shoulder barely registered in her brain as gooseflesh rose over her skin and the sensation of pressure pulsed at her back. She chanced a glance over her shoulder and was met with the most pissed off looking ghost she'd seen so far. There was a look of recognition on the female ghost's face, but it was gone so quickly that Callie wondered if it was something her brain had imagined. The thought disappeared as the pressure at her back waned and pounded into her head like a beating drum as her sense of consciousness warred with something that wasn't her.

Was the ghost trying to get into her body?

Oh shit.

TEN

DELILA DEWSBERRY DID not think twice when she pushed her way into her descendant's body and mind. In all her years roaming this plane, she had never wished for a corporeal body until now. Her son didn't look a day older than she remembered from all those years ago when he stood on her daughter's porch. The only noticeable difference was the air of evil that wrapped around him like the cloak his father had worn.

Delila pushed her consciousness into her young descendant and attempted to take control of her body, but the witch was powerful; much more than either she or her daughters had been. Pride swelled within her spirit as it occurred to her that her lineage had not only survived, but had thrived.

Before she could get too comfortable inside the witch's body, the push of the young woman's spirit beat against her as if trying to expel her from the body they shared. Delila dug deep and held tight until she could wrap her thoughts into the woman's brain in a melded union of shared thoughts.

Trust me, I gave my life to keep Elech from harming my family, and today will be no different, Delila thought along the shared mental pathway between her and the young witch.

Who the hell are you and what the fuck did you do to me? I can't even move my arms. The witch's thoughts assaulted Delila as she fought the woman's bodily movements.

I'm the only thing that will keep your friend alive.

Delila acknowledged the memories that flooded through the witch's memories as realization collided with confusion until the witch no longer doubted who Delila was.

His mother? Oh hell, no. Don't drag me into your crazy family drama. It's bad enough he could kill my Grams.

Your Grams is my great, great, great, Delila paused, trying to keep track of how many generations removed she and the old woman in Elech's grasp might be, then scrapped it. *You get the drift. She's one of my granddaughters.* Delila waited until she felt the witch accept the truth in her words and then she added, *As are you, darling.*

Shit.

The witch wasn't pleased, but neither was Delila. What had happened to the grace and dignity that the Dewsberry women had held fast to over the centuries? This woman was crass and rude, and if the tightness of the garments she wore was any indication, had no sense of what decent dress was. Delila flexed her spirit and was relieved when the witch's hands moved.

Finally a break. She raised the woman's hands and tested her voice.

"Elech, put down the dagger." The witch's voice sounded strange as it met her ears, but the tone of voice was unmistakable: authoritative and motherly. Delila and the witch held their combined breath as confusion, followed by understanding, washed over Elech's face.

"Mother? Is that you?" The hand holding the dagger twitched and droplets of blood trickled from beneath the point at which it pierced the woman's skin. "I thought you were in Hell with dear ol' dad." A smile crept up his face — cruel, cold, calculating.

"Elech, let the woman go." Fear spiked from the witch, but Delila tamped it down and stared at her son. She had spent the last days of her life fearful of this boy, and she refused to let him ruin the lives of the witches she had given her life to save. These were Thea's descendants, and after all that had befallen her children she would do whatever was necessary to save her lineage.

"Oh, but Mother, it's much more fun to watch her squirm. Don't you recognize her? She's surely related to us. She has your nose and eyes."

Us? squeaked the witch as she fought to regain control of her body.

Yes. Now, be still so I can think, Delila demanded along their telepathic connection.

"I'm aware she's a Dewsberry. As is that woman beside her." Delila tilted the witch's head toward the brunette woman holding fast to the older woman's hand. "She may have your hair color and complexion, but she also has my eyes and nose."

A look she interpreted as surprise flashed across her son's face and was quickly covered by satisfaction.

"So, you found yourself a witch to mate with." Delila's tone deadpanned. "How did you manage that?"

"Turns out I can be charming just like father." Elech beamed, pride shining in his dark eyes.

"And yet, here you are threatening your kin and those she loves."

"Threatening? No. I'm motivating her. Father always said it would take a female descendant to get access to the Overworld. And now I have her."

"Oh, Elech, you poor boy. So naive. You have always had the ability to walk between the planes."

The body Delila inhabited flinched on the witch's order. She didn't have long if she was going to convince Elech to leave them alone. The witch was too strong and she was fighting to regain control of her body.

"You lie." Her son paled and pressed the dagger further into the flesh of the woman in his grasp.

Delila used her last bit of strength to laugh. "If you only knew." The witch won the war between them and severed the mental tie that bound them.

As Delila's spirit was expelled from the witch's body deflated and tired, she hoped that her words would be enough to save her kin.

*****

Callie watched in horror as the trickle of blood that dripped from her grandmother's neck became a steady stream. Grams' skin paled and her pupils dilated while Callie wracked her brain for a solution.

"Salt." Jason's voice sounded so full and deep in her ears.

Callie whirled around in time to see a large bag of salt appear as if by magic in the crook of Jason's arm. He circled a hand in the air and a stream of salt grains followed as if he was the conductor of a salt marching band. He pointed a hand toward Daphne and salt sprinkled around her feet. He repeated the gestures until a full circle surrounded where Callie and he stood.

"Let go of her." Jason's voice was stern, but it took a moment for everyone in the room to realize he wasn't speaking to the devil. When Daphne shook her head defiantly, Callie watched Jason's eyes narrow. "Release." The word rumbled low and compelling and the golden ring around his brown eyes glowed. "Come." The same seductive nature of his tone washed over Callie turning her legs to rubber beneath her.

"No!" Daphne's cry reawakened Callie's better sense as she watched her friend and the salted circle slide across the room to where Callie and Jason stood. The clincher was when Grams' hand fell to her side with the resounding thud of flesh against flesh.

Daphne fell to the ground sobbing as Jason's magic dragged her to safety behind him.

"Witches!" The curse ripped from the Devil's throat, raw and angry. A shake of his head was the only warning before he moved his dagger hand and sliced across Grams' throat with the ferocity of a beast. He stepped back from Grams' body as blood poured from the deep wound and she gurgled on the mixture of blood and air, struggling to take her final breaths.

Shock kept Callie upright, but Daphne wailed behind her, cursing the devil and Jason both, as she fought to break whatever barrier held her where she laid tucked behind them.

When Grams' legs gave out, body limp, Elech ran the soiled flat edge of the blade across his forked tongue. "I'll be back for you. You can bet your life on it." He disappeared right before their eyes without any fanfare.

Whatever spell had kept Callie upright broke and she crumpled in a heap of hysterics beside her best friend. She crawled forward and was met with the resistance of an invisible force field of sorts. She turned questioning eyes on Jason as her body shook with sobs.

"Let me go. She can't lay there all alone." Callie sobbed. Daphne's hand found hers and clenched it with a death grip.

"Not until I'm sure he's gone." Jason's voice was steady, controlled, authoritative.

Callie flinched as if his words had physically struck her. He had the gall to think he could tell her what she could do? Rage ignited in the pit of her stomach. She wrenched out of Daphne's grasp and beat against the invisible barrier surrounding them. There was no give in it. None whatsoever.

"Calliope Jane you need to listen to that young man."

Startled, Callie turned and found the ghost of her grandmother clinging to the ghostly hands of Callie's mother. In her world, death may not be permanent, but that didn't keep the pain of her loss from grabbing her around the neck and strangling her like steel bands.

"Grams." It was less a cry and more a moan, and under any other circumstance, she would feel embarrassed by her overt display of emotion since she worked hard to keep her tough-as-nails facade firmly in place, but this was too much. Too much loss in one lifetime. Too much pain. Too much death.

Rage boiled under the surface and burst through her body, erupting in a surge of power she didn't know she had. The shelter Jason had magicked popped like a bubble on a sharpened blade of grass and the ring of salt dispersed into every corner of the sitting room.

"What the heck? I thought you didn't have power?" Jason stepped back from her, concern etched on his face as he put himself between Callie and a stunned, speechless Daphne.

"I don't know." Callie shook her head and looked around the room. The few pieces of furniture were intact, but all the pictures hung tilted on the wall as if a great wind had carried them on its current. She looked back at her hands as her mind raced. They looked the same as always, but there was no denying what she had witnessed.

"Look, if you have that much ambient power at your fingertips, than you are exactly what she needs." Jason cocked his head back at Daphne, who sat openmouthed on the floor. "We need to take her someplace safe. Sacred. And since those pendants are no longer going to keep her hidden from the damn devil, we'll concoct something that will."

Callie moved her mouth to argue, but no words came out.

"Trust me."

Jason offered his hand and she tried to read anything into the look on his face. Nothing rang the warning bells in her mind, so she put her hand in his.

And that's when she knew. He was her destiny.

ELEVEN

THE FIRST OFFICER on the scene introduced himself as Charlie Latham and gave her a knowing nod as he released them from the scene and handed her his business card. Callie wasn't sure what Charlie was, but he was more "other" than human, and being the owner of an occult shop gave her some insight to all the "others" that inhabited the town of Belvidere and the surrounding areas. Her family's shop seemed to draw them in.

Even in her state of upset, Daphne stopped and stared in openmouthed appreciation at the perfect male specimen that was Charlie. He was built like an action movie star with strong cheekbones, sandy blond hair, and was at least six-six. Add a badge and a gun to that, and he was kinda the whole package.

"Girls, we need to get a move on." Even as a ghost, Grams was both bossy and right. "Let's get Daphne to the farm. My mother always said there was no safer place than that old barn." Grams drifted ahead of them toward Callie's truck, but paused at the door, confusion etched on her ghostly face. "Oh, and don't forget those journals we brought," she called over her ghostly shoulder.

Callie watched as her mother drifted beside her grandmother and placed one hand on her in reassurance while she demonstrated with the other the capability to go right through the solid door. By the time Callie had gathered the bag of books from Charlie's crime scene and joined Daphne in the cab of the truck, both ghosts were whispering in hushed tones in the backseat with one fully solid Jason seated between them.

"What happened back there, and how did he," Daphne stuck a thumb over her shoulder toward Jason, "come out of my window?" It was the first time she had spoken since Thirteen had showed up in the B&B.

Callie pulled the truck into the light flow of traffic. She chanced a glance at her friend in the passenger seat and was not surprised to see her hands trembling and face ashen. How many times could Daph go up against the devil and keep walking away with her life? Surely there had to be a guardian angel sitting on her shoulder looking out for her. But losing Grams at Thirteen's hand had to be worse than what had happened with Daphne's mom, Hope. At least Hope was still alive, even if she appeared comatose in a care facility in the next town over. Add to that the beautiful stained glass window shattering and a grown man stepping out of the shards and it made complete sense that Daphne was questioning her sanity.

Callie glanced in the rearview mirror at her ghostly relatives and Jason and smiled. "I sorta got possessed; if that's a real thing. I'm almost positive it was Thirteen's mom." She patted her friend's leg and merged onto the main road. "Oh, and that guy's Jason. He was the smart-ass living in your window. A witch cursed him there — or so he says."

Jason piped up from the backseat and Callie shushed him as she glanced at Daphne. "You know Grams is okay, right?"

"Are you sure? I mean — I know you've been seeing ghosts, but really?" A note of hope rang in Daphne's voice.

"I'm positive. In fact, she's in the backseat with mom right now. I'm pretty sure they're talking about him." She arched her head toward Jason, smiled, and shook her head. Her life was a heck of a lot more interesting today than it had been even a few days ago. "Oh, and she told me we had to stop ogling Charlie." Callie quirked an eyebrow at her friend and steered the truck around a curve in the road.

"If he ever wrote a missed connection ad, I'd not only start reading them, but answer it." Daphne glanced over her shoulder before dropping her voice to a low whisper. "Heck, I'd be all over that if he was interested in me. Did you see how he took charge of everything back there?"

"Yeah," Callie fought unsuccessfully to keep the dreamy note out of her voice. "He was something special…" She trailed off and her imagination took over, conjuring images of the hunk and her in a twisted tangle of sheets and pillows. "Something special indeed."

"You know I can hear you back here, right?" Jason chastised, and the man in her imagination shifted to the dark haired man in the backseat.

Heat rushed through Callie's body and she waved his words away with a flick of her wrist, then pulled off onto River Road. The road was paved unlike some of the other roads in Harmony, but it was still a twisted mess of turns and potholes that wound along the Delaware River.

Daphne's phone chirped in her purse as Callie steered the truck around a hairpin turn in the road.

"What?"

Not her friend's usual cheery greeting which could only mean it was one of two people on the other end of the line.

"Don't you dare ask me questions like you have the right, you bastard. You're lucky the body bag you saw coming out of the B&B wasn't me."

Ah, so it was Dax. Callie's teeth clenched against the bitterness that coated her tongue. "Please thank your asshole of a brother for almost getting us killed. Oh wait, he did get Grams killed," Callie retorted and banged a fist on the steering wheel.

"Calliope Jane," her grandmother scolded from the backseat.

"Yeah, yeah. But it's true. That bastard stole my necklace and now you're dead," Callie whined.

"But I'm not gone," Grams reasoned.

"Sure, but you're dead as far as the rest of the world is concerned, and if I put on the necklace, you'll be dead to me, too."

A chill seeped through her, starting at her shoulder as if her grandmother had placed a hand on her shoulder from the backseat. "You can't get rid of me that easily, Calliope Jane."

After another sharp curve in the road, Callie spotted the crooked sign that indicated the road to her family's old farm property. The house was old and had been added onto over the years. The majority of the acreage sold off until it was down to a scant ten acres complete with an old barn. But it still resembled what it must've looked like a hundred or more years ago.

"Why are we coming here?" Daphne gave Callie a puzzled look. "Oh shit. I forgot Gramps. He's going to be so upset."

Dread slithered up Callie's spine. She, too, had forgotten about her grandfather. The idea of breaking the news to him gave her an instant stomachache. She pulled the truck to a stop in the middle of the gravel road, jumped from the cab, and ran to the side of the road. Stomach acid burned her throat as it raced from her body with quaking tremors. Her grandfather knew the Dewsberry history. Heck, he had agreed to take the name years ago, when it wasn't fashionable for men to do such a thing, and he had dutifully run the Daily Dews for years without complaint. But the idea of telling him that his wife had died at the hands of the beast that haunted the family for years, and had possibly taken his only daughter, was too much. Another round of tremors accompanied the remaining contents of her stomach as they poured onto the grassy roadside.

"You don't have to do this alone." Jason knelt beside her and pulled her hair back from the side of her face. "We'll do it together."

"You don't even know me. Why are you helping me?"

"I feel I owe you a favor or two, since you did get me out of that window." He gave her a crooked smile and tipped a pretend hat in her direction.

"It wasn't me that broke you out of the window," she argued. "I'm not sure who, or what, did that, but it sure as heck wasn't me."

"Oh, trust me, it was you. I haven't seen a witch powerful enough to dispel my protection bubble since Teresa. Of course with her, I didn't have enough time to get it fully solid before she threw me in the damn window. But what I saw out of you today?" He whistled. "It was some *serious* magic. The kind of magic a guy like me would be drawn to, even if you didn't look like that."

Stunned, Callie bolted upright and out of his grip.

Jason laughed. "Come on, don't pretend you think you're anything less than beautiful."

"This is so *not* the right time for this," Daphne piped up through the open truck window, making Callie jump. "We have a devil to deal with, remember? The two of you can see if you have a love connection after we figure out a way to send Thirteen back to Hell where he belongs."

Thoroughly chastised, Callie gathered her bearings, forced her feet to move back to the idling truck, and willed her head not to turn back to look at Jason. He was handsome in a timeless sort of way, which made complete sense, since the man was well into his eighties, although he only looked like he was in his early twenties. She shook thoughts of Jason from her head and focused on what still lay before her. First up, telling Gramps that his wife was gone. Like a lead balloon, dread formed large and hard in her gut. And just like that, she was back on task with pinpoint-focus on finding a way to win a war with the damn devil.

TWELVE

CALLIE WALKED INTO the farmhouse where her grandparents lived with the express purpose of rehashing Grams death with her Gramps. Every second of of her retelling felt like an infected boil on Callie's skin. Gramps reacted to the news in the way anyone might who had been told their beloved wife of almost fifty years had been killed by a devil. By the time their collective tears were dry, it was getting dark. Together, the living, newly living, and the deceased all made their way to the old barn at the back of the property.

The aged pulley system on the door refused to budge under Jason's strength. Gramps joined in the futile effort, but even their combined strength wasn't enough to move the old door. The men stepped back, Jason took Callie's hand, held it fast, and began to whisper spell-like words until the wood shuddered under the influence of his magic.

"How'd you do that?" Callie asked, eyes transfixed on the slowly moving door.

"You did it. I just tapped into your power to make it happen," Jason answered. "I've never felt so much power in one person before." His words held the hint of awe as the confession slid from between his lips; lips he pressed on the inside of her wrist before releasing her hand.

Shaken, Callie stepped away from him and entered the musty barn with Daphne on her heels muttering how hot Jason was under her breath. Grams' ghostly presence followed behind them, shushing the entire time while Gramps stepped carefully over debris scattered on the dirt floor.

"Your Grams always said there was a room back here that her mother told her to stay out of. Something about it not being the proper place for a kid to be playing, but I know she used to store stuff back here that your dad..." Gramps pointed to Daphne, "had asked her to keep out of the store." He pulled a key ring out of his pants pocket and found the key that fit into a padlock secured to a latch on a door.

All of them crowded into the small room that looked like it had once been a workshop or maybe a storage room. It was large enough for them all to squeeze in, but the light wasn't bright enough to find the books Grams babbled about as her hands went through everything she aimed to touch. After Callie reminded Grams for the third or fourth time to stop trying to touch things, a sob choked Gramps and he excused himself from the room.

"I'll go with him," Daphne offered and followed his hasty retreat.

With a little more room to move around, Callie and Jason went to work looking through everything Grams pointed at, but nothing seemed to be what they needed. After hours of kicking up dirt from the floor and dust from everything they touched, Callie wanted to quit. She stomped her feet and threw down the book in her hand, sending fresh clouds of dirt into the stale air.

"We will find it," Jason reassured.

"Find what? We aren't even sure what we're looking for," Callie whined. She wanted to tear through everything. Heck, she wanted to spell the damn books to tell her what she needed to know. She needed a breath of fresh air and some distance between her and Jason.

She wandered out of the barn and down to the pond that sat near the rear of the property. Even as a young girl, her grandmother hadn't let her go swimming in this pond. Instead, they had installed a swimming pool for when they stayed here, not that it had been often, since her grandparents moved into the apartment over the Daily Dews after her parents had died. Even on a nice summer day like today, there wasn't even a goose to be found swimming in the pond. Callie kicked the toe of her flip-flop against a rock and wiggled it free from the ground with her fingers. She needed to throw something, hit someone, or just have a plain old cry. Hell, maybe she needed to do all three, but, for right this moment, throwing the rock would have to do. She juggled the weight of the stone in her hand, pulled her arm back, and let the stone fly.

It sailed through the air and landed with a satisfying thud in the water, but didn't leave a ripple pattern in its wake.

"What the hell?"

"The pond is dead."

The voice of yet another ghost sent Callie jumping out of her flip-flops. She turned and was face to face with the ghost that had taken over her body at Daphne's.

"Oh no you don't. You are not jumping into my body again," she warned as she backed away from the ghost and edged closer toward the pond.

"Stop!" A look of panic lit sparks of life in the ghost's dead eyes.

"What?" Confused, Callie stood still while her heart rapid fired in her chest and gooseflesh rose on her arms.

"The pond. Don't go in there." The ghost widened the distance between them and motioned with her arm for Callie to come closer. "I died in that pond ages ago completing a spell that locked all the planes. If another Dewsberry witch were to die in there, it could undo everything."

"Who said anything about dying? Stepping into a pond never killed anyone." Callie shook her head, kicked off her shoes, and stepped closer to the water's edge. She was damn sick and tired of everyone telling her how the world had to be. Thirteen telling her she had to turn over her best friend or lose more of her family. Jason telling her she had enough magic to go up against the devil and succeed. Grams telling her she had to stay in town and take over the store instead of following her dreams of singing on Broadway. This was the last damned straw. She wasn't about to let some long-dead ghost of an ancestor tell her she couldn't dip her toe into the water. It was hot and she was covered in dirt and grime, and all she wanted was to wash something about this horrible day away.

Callie ignored the ghost's protests and swirled her big toe into the water; water that felt more like Jell-o: thick, dense, and not the least bit refreshing. It pulled at her skin, as if it was made of tiny little fingers, all grabbing at her and holding her there. She yanked her foot, but nothing moved other than the rest of her body, which fell to the ground in a graceless heap of skin and bones, thanks to her violent weight shift.

Beside her the ghost tsk-ed. "I warned you. Now we need to get someone out here with one of those pendants I made. It's the only thing that will get you out of there."

"You've got to be kidding me," Callie groaned. "You're the witch that made the pendants?"

"Yes. I'm Delila Dewsberry. Mother to Drammelech. I'm the one who cursed him to this plane and his father to the Underworld."

"His father?"

"Yes. Elech's father, Dema, is the ruler of the Underworld. Humans call him the devil, and I made the mistake of falling in love with him." The ghost's head sank in shame. "We had a falling out and he turned Elech against me. Only I did not realize until too much damage had already been done."

"And those pendants were to protect us from him, right?"

"Yes." Life sparkled in her eyes. "You must be descendants of my daughter, Thea, which would explain why you were named Calliope, since that was the name of her favorite sister when my children were growing up." The ghost met Callie's eyes and took a good hard look. "You remind me so much of my girls." If a ghost could be wistful, this one was nailing it.

"So, what happens if Elech got ahold of one of the pendants?" Callie tugged again at her foot, only to find it had sunk further into the mush and was now less moveable.

"He can't! If he gets a pendant, the spell that hides our descendants from him..." Delila pointed to the ground, "will be broken. And if we can't get you out of here, it'll also release Dema from his Underworld prison. I'm certain Dema won't be in a forgiving sort of mood after being trapped for over two hundred years."

Callie scratched her head and searched for the words that were most likely to get the ghost's cooperation. When nothing came to mind that sounded right, she barreled on with the cold, hard truth of the matter.

"Yeah, about that. Thirteen totally has a pendant. That's how he found us at the B&B." Delila slumped onto the ground beside her. "And it gets worse," Callie continued. "My pendant is the one he has. Grams took hers off before she died, and once we realized he could track Daphne with it, she removed hers too. I'm pretty sure they are all at the B&B which we won't be allowed back into for days until the police wrap up the investigation."

"Well, we need one of those pendants by midnight, unless you have the ability to breathe under water." And with that, Delila blinked out of sight and left Callie all alone.

"Great. That's what I was afraid of." Callie tugged her foot again when she realized the water was now up to her ankle, yet again nothing happened. She reached into her back pocket and pulled out both the business card Charlie had given her and her cell phone. She dialed the number and waited while it rang.

"Latham." His voice was clipped and low, and plucked at her nerve endings. She understood why women lined up around the block to date him.

"Hi, Charlie, it's Callie." When he said nothing, she added, "From earlier. You know, at the B&B."

"Yeah, I know who you are," his tone was hushed. "I was walking away from the scene. What d'ya need?"

"A pendant."

"A what?"

"A necklace. There should be two of them in the room where, where…" she stammered.

"Gotcha. I'll see what I can do. They might be bagged and tagged already," he warned.

"Yeah, about that, how did you convince them we weren't murderers?"

"If I told you, I'd have to kill you. As of right now, it's being investigated as a B&E gone wrong. Don't ask too many questions and keep Daphne from answering the phone when we call. As far as we know, she's out of town and won't be back until next week. Right?"

"Um, sure." Callie agreed. "Whatever you say, as long as you can get me one of those pendants soon."

"I'll see what I can do. Bring it to the Dews?"

"No. See that's the thing. I'm out here at my grandparents' old farmhouse in Harmony and I'm sorta stuck."

"Stuck how?" She could hear the dubiousness in his voice, and it cemented her belief that there was a whole lot more to Charlie than the lickable muscles and those fantastic bedroom eyes.

"Let's just pretend you won't think I'm crazy when I tell you there's a pond on the property with a magical quicksand complex. And let's also pretend you won't think I'm completely batshit crazy when I tell you I didn't listen to my dead ancestor's warning when she told me not to go into said pond. And let's pretend when I tell you I'm stuck in the pond with it slowly pulling me in, you'll believe me and do whatever it takes to get your hand on one of those pendants I asked you about, because they're kinda like the branch that will pull me out of this alive. Oh, and keep the Devil in Hell. Because, yeah, me dying here could let the Devil out of Hell." She paused to catch her breath and hoped with everything in her that Charlie wouldn't burst out laughing.

It took a solid minute before he said anything, but the words he uttered were pure music to her ears.

"I'm sending someone who can help." He took a breath and lowered his voice further, "But we're negative on the pendants. They're already in evidence and there's some things even I can't do."

"Shit. No one can pull me out of here — do you understand that? And there won't be a crime scene here because my body will never resurface."

"Trust me. I know what I'm doing."

"Charlie, I don't think you're hearing me right. There is nothing that will get me out of here besides one of those pendants." The telltale buzz of a disconnected line was all she got in response.

She swore under her breath and set the card and phone on the grass beside her.

"I thought I heard you over this way." Jason sat on the ground beside her and picked up her phone. "I've always wondered how these things worked." He fingered the device, examining it up close from every angle. "It's amazing how things have changed over the years. I mean take you for example." He waved a hand over her body, clad in shorts and a tee from a Killer's concert. "In my day, women dressed like women, but you make manly clothes look good."

"Well, take a good look, because I've been told that I'll probably die tonight."

"What?" Confusion clouded Jason's angular face. "We will find the spell to protect you and Daphne from that devil."

"Well, that would be great, but maybe you didn't notice, I'm sorta stuck here." Callie waved a hand toward her leg where the water had oozed up her calf a bit like oil coating a seabird during an oil spill.

"That's not good. I've never seen water do that before." Jason touched her leg right above the water and tugged. Nothing happened.

She already knew it would be the case, but she did take a moment to revel in the feel of his hands on her bare skin. He released her leg and stood. With hands raised in the air like a bad T.V. evangelist, he began chanting. Was that Latin? Callie sighed and settled in for the long haul.

After however long it took for the water to overtake her knee and put her other leg at such a bad angle to stay untouched, she was ready to just slide her whole body in and get on with dying. Jason kept chanting to no avail, and only stopped when her cell sounded with all the subtlety of an orchestra of electric guitars.

"What in the world is that noise?" Jason wrinkled his nose and looked around for the cause.

Callie picked up the device and hit the talk button. "Hello?"

"Is this Callie?" A woman's voice was on the other end of the phone.

"Yup. At least for a little bit longer it is."

"Good, then I made it in time. Where on the property is this pond that Charlie was talking about?"

"Oh, you're the person Charlie sent? I'm sorry to have wasted your time, but I'm pretty sure there isn't much you can do here."

"Just let me see to that, m-kay? Now, where is the pond? I see a barn, is it near there?"

Callie looked up and saw a cloud of dirt rising up from the drive that led from the house to the barn. "Keep going past the barn and you'll see it once you crest the little hill." She watched as a bright orange sedan approached.

"I see it!" The woman sounded positively giddy. "I'll see you in just a jiff, m-kay?"

Callie watched as a motherly-looking woman practically rolled out of the car door and sprang upright. Her chocolate-colored hair hung in tight curls around a sun-kissed face and framed the biggest ruby red lips she had ever seen. When the woman came close, Callie nearly fell into the deep pools that were her big blue eyes. They were amazing.

"Hi, I'm Rainee." The woman stuck out her hand and waited a beat before pulling it back. "So, Charlie says you might need a little help with your peevish pond."

"That's an understatement," Callie agreed as she stared mesmerized by the utter redness of the woman's mouth as she talked.

"Well, leave it to me and we'll get you unstuck in a jiffy, m-kay?"

Callie watched as the woman knelt at the water's edge and placed her hands above the water.

"Don't put them in there or you'll end up like me," Callie warned.

"Pish posh. I've never met a body of water that I couldn't tame." Rainee closed her eyes and laid her hands on top of the watery surface.

Callie sat horrified, refusing to breathe while the water and Rainee's hands joined together in a way that made Callie question where one stopped and the other started.

"What is she doing?" Jason whispered in Callie's ear. "Doesn't she understand that this is no ordinary pond?"

"I haven't the foggiest clue." As the words left Callie's mouth, Rainee's body turned translucent and streamed into the pond. As if her body was water. What the hell?

"Oh, that can't be good," Jason muttered as Rainee's clothes fell to the grass empty.

"Shit." Callie pointed toward the center of the pond where it looked like something was moving beneath the water. "There's something in here." Panic sent her voice up a few octaves and she struggled against the water's hold on her leg. "Get me the hell outta here."

Jason grabbed her arms and pulled. Hard. Her shoulders ached and her fingers cramped as they dug into his flesh. She was not about to get eaten alive by a pond monster.

Jason doubled his efforts and pulled even harder until she thought her shoulders would dislocate. Without warning, the water released her and she and Jason tumbled in a tangle of limbs on the grass.

"What just happened?"

"I couldn't tell you if I wanted to." She shook her head. The next moment a wave rose out of the pond, carrying what appeared to be a pile of well-preserved bones; Delila's bones if Callie had to wager a guess.

The wave washed up on shore away from Rainee's clothes and slowly morphed into the curvy shape of Rainee, big red lips and all, but totally naked.

"The water was keeping her safe. It just needed to be reassured that we would give her a proper burial." The woman reached a hand down as if to pet the surface of the pond.

"How'd you do that?" Callie asked, awe hanging on every syllable.

"We all have our little secrets, don't we?" Rainee winked as she dressed.

Callie nodded. "Did taking her bones out of there break the spell?"

Jason edged toward the pond and raised his hands again. "I'm not sure. I can still feel magic at work here."

"Okay. So, you stay here with Daphne in case Elech comes here and I'll go back to the Dews. I remember Grams telling me about a blade that can bend anything to the wielder's will. I always thought it was a legend, but after everything I've seen today, it has to be real."

"Are you sure you will be okay alone?" Jason fiddled with his fingers as if counting off things in his head, then finally threw his arms around Callie in a tight hug. "I don't feel good about sending you off this property unprotected," he said as he nuzzled the top of her head with his cheek.

"I'll be okay. I doubt Thirteen will be waiting for me at the Dews. Worst case, I'll try that spell you used at the B&B earlier. I'm pretty sure I can remember it." She ducked from under his chin, rose to her tiptoes, and planted her lips firmly on his. Electric tingles ran through her like a current looking to be grounded.

"After that, you better come back to me in one piece." His voice dropped one seductive octave and wrapped around her heart. "I knew from the moment you acknowledged me in that window that you would be the best thing that ever happened to me, and you just confirmed it." He grabbed her around the waist and kissed her again, this time slow and deep with tantalizing promises of more to come.

Walking away from him was the hardest thing Callie did all day, and it had been one of the hardest days of her life.

THIRTEEN

"COME ON, CALLIE, you know I didn't want this to happen. She's my sister. All I wanted was a chance to take what my father did and make it right." Dax paced the entryway of the Daily Dews, agitation clung to his solid frame like a cloak. Each footstep became more predator-like and each flick of his hands came closer and closer to ending with the destruction of whatever got in their way.

Callie moved out of his way, pressing herself into an overstuffed bookshelf. Had she known there was a chance she'd run into him here, she might've taken Jason up on his offer to come along. Although that could've turned whatever this was into something much worse. "The man I used to know didn't have a duplicitous bone in his body."

He stopped his momentum and swung around to face her. "See. You understand. I had no idea this would let all hell loose and send the damn devil right to you guys." His eyes pled with hers.

"I know," she soothed, but kept a safe distance from the man she had once loved. "I know you would never intentionally cause this hurt."

His hands reached for her and she resisted the urge to flinch. It was too important to let him believe that this disaster and Grams' death wasn't his burden to carry. His touch landed on her bare skin with the familiarity of a stranger. She forced down the bile that rose in her throat and pasted a smile on her face. It was the best she could conjure under the circumstances.

"You know I love you, right?"

Goddess, it killed her to look him in the eyes and nod in agreement. "But you know we can't be together, Dax. Not after everything that's happened."

His touch disappeared at her words. "I know. I wish I could change it, but you're right, nothing will ever be the same again. And for that, I'm sorry." He hung his head.

A chill ran up her spine all icicles and cold pain. Elech was coming, her body could sense him like arthritic bones could feel a storm front coming a day away. Dammit. If Dax brought him here, she would kick his ass so far into next week, he'd be able to win big in the lottery.

"What's wrong?"

"He's near." She shushed Dax with her hand and concentrated on the hum that still reverberated through her nerve endings in icy pinpricks.

"No. He can't be. He wants Daphne, not you." Whispered words hissed from Dax's lips while fear creased his brow. "He doesn't want *you*, right?" Darkness slid over his gaze. "Right, Cal? You didn't do something stupid to make him come after you, too, did you?" Every word Dax uttered grew louder until he yelled her name. "How could you be so stupid? You know what he does to people."

The accusation in his tone did little to sway her mind. She had done the right thing by coming here. Before Dax had burst through the door, she had found the book detailing the dagger and now she even had an idea how to find it; with a little help from her ghostly fairy godmothers and Jason, of course.

But if Thirteen was here for her, then she was going to get some answers. Answers he owed her. Answers she deserved after what he'd done to her family. Answers that she expected would forever change her life.

The front door banged open, sending the wind chimes that hung from the door flying through the air before they skittered across the wood floor and clanked against the front counter.

"Well, well. What do we have here?"

Elech's forked tongue snaked between his thin lips and tasted the air much like the snake in the grass that he was. His dark hair glistened in the fluorescent lights, and the shadows created by the sharp angles of his cheekbones added to the feeling of terror that washed through Callie. Her knees trembled, her hands quaked, and her resolve cracked. What had she been thinking all this time? That she could face the devil head on and walk away alive? Not likely. Not when he stared her down so close that she swore she could smell the brimstone on him.

A smile crossed the devil's face and a laugh erupted from his chest. Had he just read her mind? Oh shit, she was so screwed.

★★★★★

Drammelech relished in the temptation to end the humans standing before him. It would only serve them right for meddling in things they could never understand. The woman deserved to pay for the sins of his mother, even if she had no knowledge of them. And even though the man was one of his direct descendants, he had outlived his usefulness. And now that he held the key to unlocking his mother's curse, the man before him would only be in his way.

"Leave this place," Dax yelled, as he produced a cross from his pocket and raised it to protect his face.

Drammelech shook his head and laughed. It was funny to see what the human element believed would keep him from ensconcing with their souls. A piece of wood shaped into a symbol was only as powerful as the person who created the tool, and since most such items were manufactured en masse across the seas, they housed as much power as the air he breathed.

"Dax, don't." It was the first time Drammelech really gave the annoying woman more than a passing glance. She had hair as gold as the sun and a voice that rivaled the honeyed tones of angels. He watched with weary eyes as she tugged the cross from Dax's hands and wedged herself against the man, putting her closer to the danger that Drammelech offered.

"Callie," Dax warned.

"Don't. Just go. Meet Daphne at Grams' and have Nic meet you there, too."

Doubt colored Dax's face, but he did as told. What was most interesting was that he never once turned back to look at the woman.

"What do you want, Devil?"

The woman had moxie, Drammelech would give her that much, but as far as he was concerned, she was a fool.

"What can you offer, witch? Besides your power, which, of course, will come nicely enough with your soul."

A gasp caught in her throat and her eyes bulged. He had her right where he wanted her.

"You didn't stop to think that I would recognize the power that also courses through my veins?" His smile only pulled on one side of his mouth, leaving him with a sneer that he didn't care enough to correct. "I can feel the call of Delila in you. Almost as if she has already sunk her talons into your soul — and she has, hasn't she, witch? She was there this afternoon, not you." Drammelech watched the color drain from her face, revealing far more than he was sure she wanted known.

"Ah, so she still meddles." He shook his head. "Mother dearest never knew when to stay out of things she had no business playing in. But, if you want to hand over your soul willingly, I can promise you that I won't make you regret your existence."

"Grams warned me never to make a deal with you. In fact, she forbade it. Something about you being an asshole." The witch shrugged as challenge laced her tone.

He couldn't hold back the laugh. She was something. Something his half-sister, who she was named for, would be proud of. Fearless and frank. Hell, he almost admired her gumption.

It was too bad he was going to have to kill her.

"Look, I get it. You're the devil. You want something and I have it. Funny thing is, unlike my mother, I won't go down so easy. I'll make killing me as hard as possible, because I have something she never did... warning." She flexed her fingers at her sides and rolled up onto her toes. "I'll make it my mission to make myself hard to kill. So take your best shot, devil boy." Determination etched onto every inch of her fair skin.

"You are as foolish as my sister you were named for, witch." He growled.

"That's the thing, devil. You mistake confidence for foolery." A knowing smile spread her lips.

With a sweep of her arms, he felt magic gather in the room and surround her. A building storm washed over him, pelted into him, sank through to his core. For the first time since his mother walked the earth alive did he question his ability to control a human. He drank in the magic pummeling him and fought to clutch onto just one inkling of it to use to his advantage, but it slipped through him faster than he could process. His legs failed him, dropping him in to the floor. Who did she think she was dealing with?

Rebounding, he tapped into the magic that allowed the change. The one he swore to never complete again as long as he walked the earth. But it was either tap into that magic, or allow her parlor tricks to give her the impression of superiority. And that he wouldn't allow.

Eyes closed, Drammelech dug deep and allowed the pain that ripped him to shreds to quake through him. Around his shoulder blades, he felt the resistance of the fabric of his shirt as it split under the pressure of his emerging wings. His pants fared even worse as the bottom quadrant ripped through at the waistband and a tail sprouted forth. Intense wasn't enough to cover the implications of what transpired. Life-changing barely covered it. But like the devil he was, he rose through the hell of it and spread his wings wide. Things crashed in their wake, shattering, spilling, destruction.

The witch's face paled in earnest now and it invigorated him.

"Do you fear me now?" He pulled the dagger he kept concealed in his overcoat from the shredded fabric on the floor and brandished it.

She backed away until a bookshelf stopped her movements and the magic emanating from her collapsed. Fear. It was her weakness. Unlike his mother who had used it as an anchor, she crumbled beneath it.

"Where did you get that?"

"This old thing?" He rolled the handle between his hands. "I've had it since I was a child. Before mommy dearest locked me from entering the Overworld, I made a trip." Warmth spread through him. "I happened across a very bored darling of a gatekeeper and convinced her to part with this tool."

"That's Fate's dagger," the witch whispered. "It gives its owner the power to determine another's fate."

"That is does," he agreed. "It also is the one thing that can be the end of one of my kind. Isn't that what you're thinking, witch?"

She blanched. Her unease added to his bravado.

"But you know what else it can do?" The joy running through his veins was enough to make him giddy. "It can make a witch like yourself bend to my every whim." A single brow rose. "And let me count the ways I could use someone with your power."

He watched thoughts roll across her face: fear, determination, panic, fear again. When her feet shifted with them, he lunged. All it would take would be a flesh wound to have her under his control. The blade sliced across the softness of her abdomen. He withdrew the blade, satisfied with the red river of blood that spread across her shirt and trailed down to her waistband. With this one act, he had exactly what he needed to have it all, revenge, glory, redemption. It would be his father's undoing and his accomplishment. His legacy began here. Now. With this one injured witch.

The End

BETRAYED SNIPPET

DID YOU GET *Betrayed* by Dema? If not, read a snippet now.

BETRAYED

ONE
EARLY 1700'S

DELILA DEWSBERRY LIVED a simple life. It didn't mean that it was an unhappy life, but it wasn't a particularly fulfilling one either. As was the custom of the time, Delila had been married before she could slip too far into her teens and be too old for the task, which left her with years of experience in darning, butter churning, and child rearing. Although, these skills didn't give her the satisfaction she had dreamed her life would provide.

Her husband, Thomas, was a reputable man with a well-producing farm and a rotund midsection. Her parents had made the deal with little consideration for her opinion on the matter, but here she was living the life she'd been dealt by Fate, or God, or God-forbid the Goddess.

Delila didn't dare think the word Goddess too often, and she never uttered it aloud. In superstitious times like these, the mere mention of a being other than God would get you stoned, or worse, burned at the stake; and knowing her husband the way she did, Delila knew he would be the first to light the pylon. So Delila kept her beliefs, and her gifts, to herself. Not even Thomas, who slept beside her every night, would guess there was more to her simple life. On solstice nights, she snuck from her bed to perform the spells that kept the land fertile and the livestock well fed. Without her gifts, the farm would have turned into a worthless plot of land long ago.

Soon it would be time to celebrate the date of their betrothal. If Delila had her way, she'd be with child again soon. It did not matter how often she begged for Thomas to take advantage of his marital rites in the last three years, he always balked at the idea. Which is why she had taken to be-spelling him on their anniversary so that she could have one night of passion. Besides, if there was ever a time her husband should want her, she believed the anniversary of their betrothal was it. The need was worth the risk of being discovered a witch.

Their one night of passion was worth the risk of the stockade to combat Delila's loneliness that spanned the other three hundred sixty four nights of the year. It hadn't always taken such lengths to get her husband to notice her, but after stumbling upon Thomas and a farm hand in a passionate embrace, it had become routine for him to turn her away night after night. The allure his lover offered to Thomas had become a constant and growing source of discontent in Delila's life. On more nights that not, she yearned for something more; something greater than her current predicament could offer. Fortunately for her, and Thomas as well she supposed, she developed a new tincture that she believed would finally not only make him amorous, but also produce a child. If all went according to her plan, not only would a child breathe new life into her marriage, but also send Thomas's lover back to wherever he had come from with the outward proof of Thomas and Delila's coupling.

Delila added an extra pinch of powdered oyster to the tincture she ground together and smiled. She had often asked Thomas to convert the extra room out in the barn into a place where she could play with the tools of her father's trade, shaping ordinary things into wearable art, but he always scoffed. To Thomas, a woman's place was in the home caring for her children, not out in some barn whittling hours away on something that men did. So, while he worked, she stole away to the barn and did as she pleased in a makeshift workshop, hopeful that he would never learn of her deception.

With the exception of his infidelity, Thomas was very devout in his beliefs. Beliefs that raised their sons to be God-fearing men and their daughters to be man-serving wives.

Fifteen years into their sham of a marriage, Delila was tired of being a mother to babies, but babies were the only reason Thomas would take her to his side of their marital bed and make her feel whole. The kind of whole she dreamed of being; feminine, purposeful, powerful. To have that she would do what society dictated as conventional. She'd have children and look after a man who loved another; until the man of her dreams came for her, and come for her he would. At least, she hoped he would. This late in her life she often wondered if the mystery man who had wandered through her dreams since childhood, beckoning her to join him, was nothing more than a dream. A dream that promised love, laughter, and excitement. It was those visions that drove her forward, closer to him.

Her destiny.
Her escape.

Available now for purchase on Amazon, iBooks, Nook, & Kobo.

SACRIFICED SNIPPET

Did you get *Sacrificed* to Dema? If not, read an excerpt now.

SACRIF|CED

ONE

DRAMMELECH DEWSBERRY HAD wandered through every inch of New Jersey for over two hundred years; angry, bitter, tired. Over the years, he'd left a trail of bodies in his wake; pretty young things, all with their veins turned black. That was until he happened upon a witch—a witch who would get herself into all kinds of trouble if she were any more obvious about her magical goings on.

It was her blatant disrespect for the rules that first caught his eye, however. She stood outside a candy shop in the small town of Belvidere, offering samples to anyone who wandered by. That in and of itself wasn't anything special, but the silent spell she wove with her fingers every time someone took a morsel that compelled them into the store was very special indeed. Anyone who watched from a distance could witness the fingers on her free hand twitching in mesmerizing patterns beneath the silver tray she held.

Her movements had caught his eye on his first day in town, ensnaring him. The next day, he walked around the town square hoping to catch another glimpse of her. By his third time, she had emerged from the store with her tray, fingers dancing. It took stones to pull off magic like that out in the open, and Elech couldn't resist the draw of a woman with enough gumption to try it. He strode right up to the dark haired beauty and basked in the glow of her aura.

"Would you care to try a nut cluster?" Her voice was soft, breathy, and light. His stomach growled, full of a hunger that food would not satisfy.

"Don't mind if I do." He selected a chocolate from her tray, brought it to his nose for a tentative sniff, then popped it into his mouth. He could feel the impact of her spell as it collided with the explosion of chocolate and cashews mixed with a liquor of sorts on his tongue.

"Mmmm." He flashed her his most wicked smile and savored her offering. He nodded to her with a tip of his hat and began to walk away. "Good day."

"Sir? Wouldn't you care to go inside and purchase some more?" she called after him.

He turned back to her. "No. I think I've had just enough, witch. Unless you can offer me something a little more compelling to lure me in." He lifted his left hand and mimicked the motions of her fingers.

Her face paled and the hand holding the tray of chocolates shook. "I don't know what you're talking about." Her voice no longer held the sweet and innocent tone he'd come to identify with her in his short time watching her. Instead, it whipped at him, abrasive and full of accusation.

"Call me Elech. What do I call you?"

The woman made another sweeping gesture with her fingers, narrowed her eyes at him, and responded. "Cecily. Cecily Barren."

Elech moved to her, withdrew the tray from her hand, and set it on the open window's ledge.

"Well, Cecily, have I got a deal for you." He crooked a finger at her, beckoning her to follow him.

Available now for purchase on Amazon, iBooks, Nook, & Kobo.

FIRE'S REVENGE SNIPPET

IF YOU THOUGHT Elech's evilness could only be contained to one series, you'd be wrong. Take a peek into *Fire's Revenge*, the first novel in a series featuring elementals, witches, and our favorite devil.

FIRE'S REVENGE

ONE
OVERWORLD
CIRCA 1725

Fate knew her job as pseudo-deity was important and she took it as seriously as a being in the Overworld could. That was until, one half-devil-half-witch waltzed into the Overworld uninvited and stole a precious artifact.

With a charming face and smooth talking words, the young devil-witch dazzled Fate. It had been so long since the last time she had actually conversed with another. The ideas of a visit from a being that could walk through the veils that kept humans from the Overworld and Underworld played on her heartstrings; played them like a master composer.

Their time together was brief. In his first visit she only learned his name: Drammelech; Elech as his family called him. She offered him her title in lieu of her name: Fate. He had flashed her a wide smile with the hint of a dimple at its corner and said that she must have known he'd come for her. She laughed off his flirty nature and relished the time they spoke.

He brought her a single fluffy pink flower on his next visit.

"What is this?"

"Rue."

"Rue? Why would you bring me something with such a sad connotation attached to its name?" Fate studied the young man before her.

"Because I rue that I cannot have you in my everyday life. Your beauty speaks to me in a way that nothing in my realm ever has." Bashful eyes lowered, punctuating his proclamation with the light stain of red that colored his cheeks.

It was in that one simple confession that her heart filled as it never had before. She took great pains to make sure every moment of their time together was well spent; full of laughter, conversation, and genuine happiness. On one particular visit, when Elech asked to see more than the main chamber of her Overworld post, she didn't hesitate before taking him into her most favorite room; the records room.

She led him into the vault where every being's scroll was kept under lock and key. It reminded her of the warehouses that her charges were so keen on using to store useless baubles and tokens. The difference was that this chamber was unending.

The day she had taken over for the previous soul, she had been shown into this very chamber of vastness that seemed larger than anything she could comprehend. She recalled asking in a hushed tone how big the chamber was. The look on her predecessor's face was enough of an answer that no more words had been needed.

In her years, she had tried to understand the organization of the vast room, but she had yet to figure out the magical system to the order of the scrolls. Although, the easiest to find belonged to the mystical beings which lived among the humans. Those scrolls always appeared near the front of the shelves and often had brightly colored symbols on the exterior of the rolled parchment.

With every falling grain of sand in the constantly flowing hourglass that mimicked the time of her charges, scrolls would appear or disappear as if they had always been as they were with the next drop. She oftentimes wondered if the disappearing scrolls reappeared elsewhere in the cavernous chamber, but to venture forth in search of them would take longer than she could spare. In the turn of her back, turmoil could erupt amongst her charges since time in the Overworld didn't work the same as it did on Earth. With that in mind, her forays into this chamber were typically the highlight of her time spent in the Overworld.

Fate stepped aside and allowed Elech into this sacred space. It gave her a sense of joy to be able to share this place with someone. The majestic nature of it all never failed to take her breath away and she wanted so much to see her joy reflected in his piercing eyes. She watched, rapt, as a wash of emotions rolled over his handsome face.

"What is this place?" Awe laced every word.

"I call it the chamber of records." She fingered the delicate shell of the hourglass. "This is where the universe balances. Within the scrolls, there is a tenuous balance struck between light, dark, old, new, beginnings, and endings."

Elech walked farther into the room and ran a hand along a row housing mounds of scrolls. His fingers settled on one and slipped it from the shelf. With gentle fingers, he unrolled the parchment and scanned it.

"What if this scroll were to get misplaced?" He rerolled the record and held it between his thumb and forefinger like it might burn him.

"It mustn't." Fate moved toward him and snatched the scroll from his grasp. "This single scroll represents the life of one of my charges and if something were to change, another scroll would surely appear to act as balance." She gently slid the scroll back into its place on the shelf.

Elech nodded and walked back to the main opening in the chamber. Beside the hourglass was a podium that held the largest tome the world never knew existed. Its leather wrapped spine was the glue that held all of Earth's existence together. Tucked into the pages of the book laid the blade of the most powerful item in the chamber: Fate's dagger. Her predecessor had gone to great lengths to reiterate the importance of keeping it hidden away, and now his words resurfaced in the forefront of her mind as Elech drew closer and closer to its resting place. An item of such power could be used to do so much damage in the world in the wrong hands, but in hers it was the instrument to set things gone awry on a corrected path. A sigh left her lips as Elech inspected the hourglass.

Fate watched the steady trickle of sand and moved to her left. She fingered the thick leather-bound tome that was home to a list of names and slid the jeweled silver hilt from between the book's pages. It felt heavy in her hand as she tucked it into the garter beneath her long flowing skirt. The knowledge that it was safe gave her a sense of peace.

Elech's next visit was years later even though the time passed in seemingly the blink of an eye. This time when he came to her, he appeared a full grown man even though she knew his age to still be young by her charges' standards. Instead of another pink fluffy rue, he held in his hand a long stemmed white rose.

"I thought you might've forgotten me," she remarked as she accepted his offering.

"Never."

His voice was deep, full-bodied, and sent a chill racing down her spine. When his hands slid down her arms, an actual shiver sliced through her body. How long had it been since she had felt the touch of another? Long before being assigned to her current post, that's for sure. She arched into him, pleased to find him hard and angular beneath her wanton fingers. In the space of a breath he had her in his arms, hands scorching over her exposed skin until fabric balled into his eager hands. His mouth, warm on her chaste lips, tasted like sunshine and a warm summer's breeze.

Fate threw caution and all her dignity into the wind and succumbed to Elech. With each tantalizing touch of his fingers against her flesh, she basked in the sensations of seduction. The anomaly of a fluttering in her chest that had earned her this post, kicked up as his tentative touches became more determined on their trail up her thighs beneath her skirt. She closed her eyes and cherished the intimacy of her predicament until a tug sent her eyes wide. The cool blade of the dagger she wore in the garter against her thigh sliced though her delicate flesh in a rush of warm, sticky liquid. Before she could defend herself, the press of the blade against her throat halted any further movement.

"I hate to do this," Elech whispered in her ear. "But you are the only thing standing between me and greatness." He pressed his lips to hers in a final kiss as the blade dug into her skin once more, this time slicing across her throat until it became hard to breathe. The fluttering in her chest that made her more human than ethereal catapulted, racing toward a finish line she could no longer sense. Elech stood, wiped the broad side of the blade against his trousers and blinked out of the realm.

Without her to dictate the course of human existence, chaos was sure to ensue, but protecting her charges from whatever evil Elech planned was more important. With her last breaths, she dragged herself into the chamber of records and sealed the doors behind her with all of her remaining magic. Now he would need more than just his smooth words to get into the chamber. Satisfied with her fortitude and forethought, she crumpled into a heap on the floor, knocking scrolls about on her way down. As much as she wanted to retrieve them and put them right again, she no longer had the strength. She stared at the scattered rolls of parchment, most decorated with symbols she knew instinctively. The mess on the floor would surely change the course of life for her beloved charges, but how, she could only guess.

Her last thought flashed through her brain on the fading embers of light in her soul. "What have I done?"

Available now for purchase on Amazon, iBooks, Nook, & Kobo.

WANT A SNEAK PEEK AT WHAT'S COMING

NEXT FOR ELECH?

IF YOU CAN'T get enough of your favorite devil, visit www.jeniburns.com for news regarding upcoming releases.

BIOGRAPHY

JENI BURNS is a Jersey girl living in a southern world. While she's firmly planted in the South with her husband, two kids, and one massive poodle, her heart still lives in the Northwestern part of New Jersey where her characters reside. Since writing about home is cheaper than airfare, she spends much of her time living vicariously in NJ's snowy winters and humidity-free summers.

Jeni has been telling stories since she first learned to string two words together. Thanks to her mom and her middle school English teacher both telling her she should be a writer; she now happily spends her days writing all the stories that continuously float around in her head while drinking fabulous decaf coffees.